Conspiracy

"I'm afraid to tell you everything over the phone," said Colleen.

"What's the matter?" asked Regan. "Are you afraid it's bugged."

"It might be. You never know about these things."

"Well, what do you want from me?"

"Our lives may be in danger," she said.

"How do you figure that?"
"Dave and Paul Bagdonovich may be the only two people alive who know that Lee Harvey Oswald had a different name when he was in the Marines."

"He what?" said Regan as he sat upright in the chair.

"You heard me. I've heard all those stories about a conspiracy and all those witnesses dying accidentally or suddenly. If these stories are true, then their lives, and now mine and yours, could be in danger."

We will send you a free catalog on request. Any titles not in your local book store can be purchased by mail. Send the price of the book plus 50¢ shipping charge to Leisure Books, Two Park Avenue, New York, New York 10016. Attention: Premium Sales Department.

Titles currently in print are available for industrial and sales promotion at reduced rates. Address inquiries to Nordon Publications, Inc., Two Park Avenue, New York, New York 10016, Attention: Premium Sales Department.

TWICE DEAD

Larry D. Names

LEISURE BOOKS • NEW YORK CITY

A LEISURE BOOK

Published by

Nordon Publications, Inc.
Two Park Avenue
New York, N.Y. 10016

Copyright © 1978 by Nordon Publications, Inc.

This book is a work of fiction.

The Double Oswald Theory, however, is one of many theories concerning the assassination of President Kennedy. Any resemblance to persons living or dead, with the exception of actual historical figures, is purely coincidental.

I

Cubi Point, The Philippines

March 10, 1959

Ellis David O'Toole, corporal, United States Marine
Corps, entered his barracks shortly after lunch. He
walked directly to his bunk, which was situated in the
middle of the long room. He was going to get a pack of
cigarettes out of his foot locker. He squatted down in
front of the locker taking the combination lock in his left
hand, but as he did, he noticed something was wrong
with his bunk. There was a wrinkle in the blanket,
which suggested to him that someone had sat on his
bunk that morning.

Who the hell has been sitting on my bunk? he swore to
himself angrily.

O'Toole dropped the lock and proceeded to smooth
out the wrinkle in the blanket. Being an extremely
meticulous person, he was truly upset by the incident.
He would make it a point to find out who had done the
misdeed.

He returned to his locker to fetch the cigarettes he
had come for in the first place. He twisted the dial with
the right combination, and the lock popped open. He
removed the lock and lifted the lid to discover that his
cigarettes were in the wrong position; the brand name
was upside down. That was strange, because he always
placed the packs with the brand name in such a position
that it could be read instantly when the locker was

5

opened.

O'Toole concluded that someone had gotten into his locker during the morning while he was at work. He was certain that someone had burglarized his possessions. He began a systematic check of them to see if anything was missing.

He counted the packs of cigarettes. All were there.

He opened his shaving kit. Razor and toothbrush were there.

His uniforms were in the right places.

Personal affects were next to be accounted for. Pen, pencil, writing tablet, letters from home. All there. Camera, radio, pictures . . . . His pictures were missing!

Why? he asked himself.

The answer was eighteen years away.

II

Glen Egan, Wisconsin

February 8, 1977

The telephone rang in the office of the *Weekly Times,* the oldest newspaper in central Wisconsin. The secretary answered the call.

"It's long distance for you, Tom," she announced in a voice loud enough for the whole crew to hear.

The regular office crew consisted of six women and two men. Only four of the women and Thomas Marshall Regan were present at the time of the call. The girls, as Regan referred to them away from the office, pretended not to be listening, but they were all ears, especially when Regan received a call. Being the products of small towns, they were always ready to overhear all conversations, particularly if the person calling Regan was a woman. Since Regan was unmarried, his personal life was open to much speculation.

"I'll take it in Barney's office," said Regan as he swivelled in his chair.

Regan pushed himself out of his chair and walked into Barney Nutter's office. The editor's private domain was supposed to be off limits when he was not around, but Regan liked to use it whenever possible because it offered him the privacy he liked when talking on the phone and because it was one of the many little ways of getting at Nutter, a boss who was rumored to be a descendant of Ebenezer Scrooge. Regan closed the door behind him and flopped down in Nutter's chair. He picked up the receiver and pushed the button below the flashing red dot.

"This is Tom Regan. May I help you?"

"Hello, Tommy, this is Colleen."

Colleen O'Toole was Regan's younger sister who lived in Tulsa, Oklahoma. The two of them saw each other infrequently, but they spoke regularly over the telephone, which usually happened when one or the other had a problem and needed a friendly ear. As brother and sister, they were about as close as two people in the same family could ever be.

"Say, little sister, what's happening in Okieville these days?"

"Not much more than what's happening up there inside the Arctic Circle," she drawled.

"Is everyone okay down there?"

"If you're asking if Mom is all right, then the answer is yes; but if you're asking about me, then the answer is no. I stayed home from work today with a strep throat, but that isn't why I called."

"Then why did you call? Someone else sick?"

"No, everyone is fine. I called because I think Dave and I have a problem."

"Sorry. I do not give advice on marital problems. That's the quickest way I know to wear out your welcome with your friends and relatives."

"It's not that kind of problem. Our lives may be in danger."

"Isn't that a little melodramatic? Who is it this time? The Mafia? A Russian spy? Or is it the lunatic down the street again?"

"I'm serious, Tom."

"Okay, tell big brother all about it."

"That's better," she sighed. "Now listen closely."

Regan knew that his sister had a penchant for exaggeration. As she began to tell him her bizarre tale, he wondered how much of it would be fact and how much would be her active imagination.

"Last night," Colleen began, "a man called and wanted to talk to Dave. I answered the phone in the bedroom, and Dave took it in the kitchen. Well, I listened in on their conversation instead of hanging up the extension. What I heard really has me worried."

"Well, tell me what you heard, and I'll decide if you have anything to worry about."

"Okay," she sighed again. "Well, this man said he was writing a book on the life of Lee Harvey Oswald. He asked Dave if he could remember anything about Oswald. Dave said he didn't know Oswald, but the man said he must have known him because Oswald was stationed with him in the Marines. Dave said he didn't know Oswald when he was in the Marines. Well, the man said he must've known him because they had been stationed at all the same places at the same times. Dave still denied knowing Oswald. Then the man asked Dave if he knew a Paul Bagdonovich, and Dave said he did. The man said that according to the records he got from the Marines, Paul, Dave and Oswald were in the Philippines at the same time in 1959 and at the same place. Dave said he had been there at that time, but he couldn't remember Oswald. Well, the man said he wanted to talk to Dave about it some more, and he asked if he could visit us when he came to Tulsa. Dave said he'd be wasting his time, but he told the man that he was welcome to come by here when he was in town."

"So what's the big deal, Colleen?"

"After the man hung up, Dave told me that he hadn't

told him the whole truth. He hadn't actually known Oswald, but he did know something about him from those days.''

"Like what?''

"I'm afraid to tell you everything over the phone.''

"What's the matter? Are you afraid it's bugged?''

"It might be. You never know about these things.''

"I guess,'' sighed Regan. "Well, what do you want from me?''

"Tommy, I wish you would come down here and talk to Dave about this thing. There's a lot more to it, and I think you're the only one who can help.''

"What do you need help for?''

"Our lives may be in danger.''

"How do you figure that?''

"Dave and Paul Bagdonovich may be the only two people alive who know that Lee Harvey Oswald had a different name when he was in the Marines.''

"He what?'' said Regan as he sat upright in the chair.

"You heard me. I've heard all those stories about a conspiracy and all those witnesses dying accidentally or suddenly. If those stories are true and what Dave thinks is also true, then all our lives may be in danger. If Oswald did have a different name and Dave and Paul are the only two people who know it, then their lives, and now mine and yours, could be in danger.''

Regan went over his sister's story for a few seconds in his head. Neither of them spoke in the interim.

"You just might have something here, Colleen. Let me think about it, and I'll call you back later. Okay?''

"Okay, I'll wait for your call.''

They said their farewells, and Regan put down the receiver. He remained seated in his boss's chair while he mulled over Colleen's story again. Before he could come to any conclusions or make any decisions about it, Barney Nutter opened the door. Regan looked up to see the editor looming over him from the doorway.

"What the hell do you think you're doing in here?" boomed Nutter.

"I was just using your phone," said Regan without rising from Nutter's chair.

"Haven't you got a phone on your own desk?"

"Yeah, but . . ."

"But shit! Get your ass out of my chair and get it back to work. At your own desk. Now."

Regan sat there glaring up at Nutter, who towered over him like some sort of beast about to devour him. Nutter leaned over a little to emphasize his command. Regan got up from the chair as he thought of a better way to settle things with Nutter.

"Pardon me," said Regan as he edged past Nutter into the outer office.

Regan took deliberate steps as he marched over to his desk, the oldest and most dilapidated one in the room. He pushed his chair out of the way as he reached up to remove his favorite cartoon from the wall where he had taped it the day Barney Nutter became the editor of the *Weekly Times*. He pulled his chair out again and sat down. He picked up a black marking pen and printed a few carefully chosen words under the cartoon's caption.

After editing the cartoon, Regan rolled his chair back from the desk, stood up, and marched himself back to Barney's office. The door was closed. He started to knock but thought better of it. Instead, he opened the door and walked in without closing the door behind him.

"Barney, I've got something here for you to read,"

said Regan as he unceremoniously handed over the cartoon with the extra Regan touch on it.

Nutter took the caricature of a beleaguered white-collar worker leaning over his employer's desk. He read the caption which had said, "You can't fire me. You have to sell slaves." Regan had edited it to say, "You can't fire me. You have to sell slaves, Nutter, but this one just got emancipated; therefore, I quit." Under the new caption, Nutter read, "Look up, Barney, but keep your mouth closed. I can't stand your filthy breath or rotten teeth."

Nutter looked up to see Regan displaying the middle fingers of his hands in upright positions.

"You already know what these mean, Nutter," said a triumphant Regan, "but did you know that your wife is the best forty-year-old piece of tail in town? Everyone else knows it."

With that, Regan grabbed the doorknob and closed the door behind him as he walked out on a life that he thought he had always dreamed of having. He went to his desk to retrieve a few personal items. He grabbed his coat and headed for the front door. Stopping in front of it, he turned around to face the girls who had been watching his every movement for the past six months.

"Well, good-bye girls," he said. "I hope the next guy to come in here is a queer. Then he won't have to worry about who screws and tells."

A moment later, Regan was in his car. His next stop would be Tulsa, Oklahoma.

III

Tulsa

February 10, 1977

Regan parked his car in the driveway of the little house on Trenton Street. He switched off the engine but remained in the seat for a moment as he stared at his mother's darkened house. He was exhausted from the long drive from Wisconsin.

It had taken him almost a complete day to tie up all his loose ends in Glen Egan. He had packed nearly everything he owned in his Toyota. He had called his sister to inform her that he was coming as she had requested. She was to expect him some time during the next two days. He had felt it would be wiser to get a good night's rest before leaving; so he spent one last night in his cluttered apartment.

The following morning he had gone to his landlady to ask for a refund on the rent he would not be using because he had no plans to return to Glen Egan. She had refused to refund any money to him. Regan decided to let it slide. He figured that she owed him half of the month's rent, and the lamp in the bedroom was worth that much. It was a fair exchange.

He had informed the telephone company to disconnect his service, and he had done likewise with the utility company. To insure that there were no more charges for services rendered beyond that day, Regan had turned off the gas and electricity himself; and he had cut a one-foot section out of the telephone cord.

The last stop on the way out of town had been the bank. He had withdrawn all but one dollar from his savings account. It had always been his belief that it was unlucky to close a savings account. It was a silly superstition, but he adhered to it almost religiously. He had filed the passbook with six others he had accumulated to that point in his life. Each one had one dollar as its last entry.

Regan had told no one in Glen Egan where he was going, nor had he left a forwarding address with the Postal Service. He had decided to leave that little midwestern town to itself. As far as Glen Egan was concerned, Thomas Marshall Regan was just another train passing through it in the night. He would never come that way again.

As he gazed at the white house in front of him, Regan wondered what kind of reception his mother was going to give him this time. She was always happy to see her second oldest son, but she was always glad for different reasons. One time she would be delighted to see him because she was broke and needed money. Another time it was because her car needed fixing. It was always something different, but she was always glad to see him.

Finally, Regan opened the car door to drag his fatigued body to the front door of the one-story house. The screen door was still broken, which meant the doorbell was probably not working either. He rapped the wooden sash with the knuckles of his right hand. His finger joints ached from pounding them too hard. He figured that he had made enough noise to wake up the whole neighborhood.

The shades were drawn over all the windows. Despite that fact, Regan could see that a light had come on

14

in his sister Laurie's bedroom. Moments after the first light's appearance, another one illuminated the living room. The shade over the living room window was peeled back by a hand with long fingers. He saw the forehead and eyes of his sister peek out at him. Her eyes widened with recognition, and the shade fell back in place.

"It's Tommy," he heard Laurie shout from inside.

"Let me in," said Regan. "It's cold out here."

The door opened in front of him. Laurie was standing behind it in her bathrobe. Regan stepped inside, and she closed the door behind him. He turned to appraise his sister's appearance. Laurie was only sixteen, but she was already taller than Regan, a fact that was due to her having had a different father. A lock of her dishwaterblonde hair was hanging over the corner of her right eye. Still possessing some baby-fat, Laurie was already a lot of woman.

"My lord, where did you come from?" drawled Laurie in an attempt to hide her pleasure at seeing Regan.

"Same place as you did, kid," said Regan, "my mother, except I came first; so show a little respect when you're talking to an elder."

"You ain't my elder," she sneered.

"You wouldn't want to bet on that, would you?"

Regan grabbed her by the wrist and pulled her toward him as he flopped down on the sofa. He caught her legs between his knees, then forced her to bend over into a spanking position. She tried to resist, but Regan was too strong for her.

"Tommy, stop it!" she cried.

He swatted her squarely on the rump.

"OW!" she screamed.

15

"Now when you're big enough to stop me from doing this, I'll stop being your elder. Do I make myself clear?"

"You better let me go."

He spanked her again.

"OW!"

"A little more respect?"

"Okay, okay!"

"What the hell's going on here?" demanded Regan's mother as she waddled into the living room from the hall.

"Just helping you fetch this kid up right, Mom."

"I don't need no help."

"I'll remember that the next time you call to cry on my shoulder about what an ungrateful little brat that Laurie is."

"I never in my life called any of my kids a brat."

"Bull!"

"You watch your mouth, boy," she warned with the same fire in her eyes that she placed in her hair.

"Why? Is it going somewhere?"

"Thomas Marshall, one more smart word out of that foul mouth of yours, and I'll tan your hide."

She looked menacing enough to do it, but Regan knew her better than that. He burst out laughing as he released Laurie from her position of punishment.

"Come here, fat lady," said Regan as he patted the sofa next to him, "and give a gool ol' boy a hug and a kiss."

"Who you callin' a fat lady?" she snarled.

"If you're going to take that attitude, I'll go stay at Colleen's."

Regan stood up as if he really intended to leave. His mother moved between him and the door.

16

"Where do you think you're goin'?"

Regan answered her by surrounding the roundness of her frame with his arms and his love. He squeezed her to him, and she reciprocated by locking her short but powerful arms around his neck.

"How are you, son?" she asked joyously.

"I'm fine, Mom," he replied as he started to kiss her.

"Hope," she said as she turned her cheek to his lips. "I told you-all the last time you was here; I don't kiss no one with a beard."

Regan laughed as he rubbed his multicolored whiskers against her cheek and neck.

"Now stop that, Tommy," she giggled. "What're you doin' here in the first place?"

"Didn't Colleen tell you I was coming?"

"That girl don't tell me nothin'. None of you kids tell me a damn thing. I'm always the last to find out what's goin' on."

"Well, I came down here to talk to her and Dave about his career in the Marines."

"Did she call you about that crap?"

"What crap?"

"That crap about Dave and Lee Harvey Oswald."

"No, what about it?"

"Did she tell you their lives were in danger?"

"Yeah, she did, but what about it?"

"It's all a lot of bull."

"Do you mean Dave wasn't in the Marines with Lee Harvey Oswald?" Regan was beginning to panic.

"No, he wasn't in the Marines with him. Colleen called me yesterday, and she said that the man who'd called Dave before called again. Dave was in a different outfit than Lee Harvey Oswald."

"Are you sure of that, Mom?"

17

"Of course, I'm sure."

"That's really great!" shouted Regan as he jumped to his feet and started to pace the room. "That's really terrific! Here I thought something fantastic was going to be found out, and I'd get to write the story about it. So I quit my job, and now there's no story. That's really fantastic! Damn that Colleen!"

"You can always get another job."

"Like hell, I can. You don't know what I said to my former employer when I quit."

"What'd you do? Tell him to go to hell or something?"

"I wish that was all I'd done."

"Well, you go sleep in my room. Everything will be brighter when the sun comes up."

"Like hell, it will. I'm going over to Colleen's right now to thank her for helping me screw up my life, as if I needed any help."

"You'll do no such thing. You're goin' in the other room, and you're goin' to get some rest."

Regan's mother was adamant on the subject, and he knew it would be senseless to argue with her. He went to his mother's bedroom, but he refused to sleep at first. He was too angry with Colleen to rest. He undressed and got into the bed to stare at the ceiling. He began rehearsing the tongue-lashing he wanted to give his sister when he would see her later that morning, but his fatigue beat down his angry spirit, forcing it to rest.

* * * * *

Regan had cooled his temper at the insistence of his mother before calling Colleen.

"Oh, Tommy, I'm so glad you're here," said Colleen. "Where are you now?"

"I'm at Mom's," he said coolly.

"Good. I'm not going to work today. So come over here right away. I've got a lot to tell you."

"Oh, really," he said sarcastically. "Like what?"

"You know; what you came here for."

"Look, Colleen, Mom told me about the second call from that man, that writer."

"I figured she would. I only told her that so she wouldn't worry. You know how easily she gets excited. I just didn't want her getting upset over this."

"Is that the truth?"

"As the Lord is my witness."

Regan knew that his sister did not take the Lord's name in vain. Whenever she called upon Him to testify to her veracity, she was telling the whole truth without exaggeration or magnification as she was often known to do.

"I bought it once, Colleen."

"Tommy," she whined.

"I guess that was just the down payment. Okay, I'll be right over."

Dave and Colleen lived on the south side of Tulsa. From his mother's house, it was a half hour's drive through heavy traffic most of the way. They lived in an apartment complex where all the buildings were exactly alike and the numbers on the doors were too small to be read from a car passing through the parking area, which made it difficult to find any particular apartment a stranger such as Regan might be looking for. Still, Regan managed to find the right building on the first attempt. He parked on the wrong side of it, but he found their apartment.

Colleen met Regan at the door with a warm embrace

and a friendly smile. He walked inside the two bedroom flat to see that it still had the same furnishings as the last time he had been there. The red and black chairs and sofa were there with the Mediterranean style tables and lamps. The pictures of the matador and the flamenco dancers were still hanging in the same places. It was as if he had only been away for a few days instead of eleven months.

Colleen had not changed in the interim either. She was still as slender as ever, which only accentuated the pointedness of her chin. Regan had always thought her nose resembled that of Bob Hope's. Even her hair-style was the same. It was still out of place on her head, especially with the blonde streaks in the wrong places in the dull brown coiffure. Her eyes were still a lighter blue than Regan's.

"Would you like something to eat?" asked Colleen.

"No, but I'll take a cup of coffee and some answers."

"Okay, I'll heat the coffee."

Colleen went around the corner to the kitchen, and Regan pulled up a chair at the table in the dining area.

"Let's get right to it, Colleen. I want to know everything that's going on here."

"Okay, where do you want me to start?"

"The beginning would be nice. Some dates, names, and places would be helpful, too."

"Okay," said Colleen as she left the kitchen and went to her bedroom. She returned a minute later carrying an old shoe box stuffed with papers. She placed the box on the table in front of Regan.

"Most of Dave's career is in there," she said as she pointed to the box. "Dates, names, and places. There's also some pictures."

Regan picked out some papers to look at, but then he

20

thought better of it.

"Before I start digging into all this, you'd better tell me what you know first."

"Okay, I'll tell you what Dave told me."

"Okay, let's have it."

"Remember I told you about a friend of Dave's named Paul Bagdonovich? Well, Dave, Paul and another Marine named Phil Schramm used to hang around together. They were real good friends till Schramm got killed in the Philippines in 1959. He was shot with his own gun while he was on guard duty one night. Dave said that the Marines said he had committed suicide. Dave didn't believe that, because the day Schramm was killed he had received a promotion and a letter from his girlfriend that said she'd marry him when he got out of the Marines."

"What's this got to do with Lee Harvey Oswald?"

"The man who was supposed to relieve Schramm the night he was killed was Lee Harvey Oswald. He's the one who reported finding Schramm's body."

"And Dave thinks Oswald killed Schramm, right?"

"Not exactly. The man who called us, the writer I told you about? Well, he called back the night I called you. He's the one who told us about Oswald relieving Schramm. The strange thing is there isn't any record of a Phil Schramm ever having been killed in the Philippines in 1959. In fact, this man told us that there isn't even any record of a Phil Schramm ever having been in the Marines, not then or ever."

"Wait a minute. If there's no record of the killing and there's no record of this Schramm, how does this guy know that Oswald was supposed to relieve him on watch that night?"

"He said Paul Bagdonovich told him that. You see,

21

Dave had been left behind in Japan when they went to the Philippines for maneuvers. He didn't get to the Philippines till the day after Schramm was killed. He didn't know anything about Oswald, but Paul Bagdonovich had been there all along and he knew everything that was going on."

"Then maybe I should talk to this Paul guy. He seems to have more answers than Dave does."

"Yeah, you should talk to him, but let me finish telling you what Dave knows first."

"Okay, go on."

"Well, a few days before they were supposed to leave the Philippines and go back to Japan, someone broke into Dave's locker and stole his pictures. The thief didn't take anything else. Just the pictures. What's stranger about it is Schramm was in most of those pictures. The thief should have taken Dave's camera, too, because he had a whole roll of exposed film in it."

Colleen dug into the shoe box in front of Regan. She removed a dozen old photographs from an envelope. She placed them in front of Regan who picked them up to look at them.

"Those are the pictures that were in the camera."

"Which one is Schramm?" asked Regan as he held up a photo of two Marines in T-shirts leaning against a bunk.

"He's not in that one."

Regan went to the next photo, which was a picture of a Marine relaxing in a bunk. He started to go to the next one, but Colleen stopped him.

"That's Schramm," she said.

"This one?" asked Regan as he held out the picture of the Marine in the bunk.

"Yes, that's him."

22

Regan studied the photograph more closely. He thought he recognized the face, but he was not certain that it was Lee Harvey Oswald in the photo smiling back at him.

"Wait a minute. This guy looks like Lee Harvey Oswald."

"That's what I thought too, but Dave insists that this is a picture of Phil Schramm."

"He must be mistaken. This is definitely Lee Harvey Oswald."

Colleen got up and went to the closet next to the refrigerator. She reached up to the shelf above the coat rack and retrieved a book. She returned to the table and opened the book to the pages that had photographs on them. The pictures were all of Lee Harvey Oswald.

"Here look at these," said Colleen as she placed the open book in front of her brother.

Regan compared the photograph in his hand to those in the book. The face of the man in the bunk matched the face of the man in some of the photographs in the book.

"See? I told you this was a picture of Oswald."

"But, Tommy, Dave insists that this is Phil Schramm in this picture. Phil Schramm who was killed in the Philippines in 1959."

"Something's screwy here. Either Dave is mistaken or . . . ."

"Or what?"

"I don't know, but something smells. Something smells like a story to me."

"That's what I think, too."

"Oh, yeah? What else do you think?"

"Well, Dave and I talked about all this, and we think Schramm's death had something to do with Oswald."

"Like what?"

"Well, Dave was one of those guys who directs airplanes. I don't remember what you call them."

"An air-traffic controller?"

"That's it. Anyway, that was his job when he was in the Marines. Well, one day when they were in Japan Dave and Paul Bagdonovich saw a U-2 plane in a hangar. Do you remember the U-2 plane incident in 1960? The one the Russians shot down?"

"Yeah, the pilot was Gary Francis Powers."

"Well, Dave said that Schramm was supposed to have seen it, too. He thinks that Oswald may have seen the same plane. Oswald was a radar operator over there. Dave thinks that he may have known about the U-2 flights and that was the information that he gave the Russians when he defected."

"I don't see the connection between Schramm's death and Oswald and the U-2 flights. How do they all tie in together?"

"Dave and I were wondering the same thing till that writer called the second time. He said that Schramm's death had been covered up and that Schramm had disappeared in all the records. He said that according to the Marines Phil Schramm never existed. Dave knew Phil Schramm and so did Paul Bagdonovich, and now this writer says that Schramm never existed."

"No, you said the writer said the Marines say Schramm never existed."

"Okay, the Marines said it, but that doesn't erase the fact that Dave and Paul knew a guy by that name. If he wasn't Phil Schramm, then who was he?"

"Maybe he was Lee Harvey Oswald."

"That's what Dave thinks."

"Wait a minute. If Schramm and Oswald were the

same person, then Oswald was an agent just like his mother said he was.''

"His mother said that he was an agent?"

"Yeah, that's what she told the Warren Commission. She said he was an agent, but she didn't know who he was working for."

"That might explain why someone stole Dave's pictures."

"Right, but I can't help but get the feeling that we're overlooking something or that something else is missing."

"Like what?"

"I don't know, but I'm sure as hell going to find out. Have you got copies of this picture?" He held up the one of the Marine in the bunk.

"No, but we still have the negative to it."

"Good. Don't lose it. It may be valuable. I'm going to need this one."

"Why?"

"To show people who may have known Schramm, alias Oswald. People like Paul Bagdonovich. Do you know where he lives now?"

"Sure. We got a Christmas card from him and his wife." Colleen went to the shoe box again. "Here it is."

Regan took the envelope from Colleen. He took a pen and a notebook from his shirt pocket. He copied the address off the envelope.

"Looks like my next stop is Phoenix."

IV

Phoenix

February 13–14, 1977

The temperature was in the seventies when Regan saw the house on Wagon Wheel Drive for the first time that Sunday afternoon. The wooden shingles on the roof were matched by the rustic wooden shutters around the windows of the white house. Citrus trees provided shade on the front lawn, which was sunken for irrigation. Regan parked his car along the rounded curb in front of the Bagdonovich residence. He walked up the driveway to a walk that led to the front door. He rang the doorbell, and a woman with platinum-blonde hair and a tanned face answered the door.

"Yes?" she said softly.

"Mrs. Bagdonovich?"

"Yes?"

"My name is Tom Regan. I'm Dave O'Toole's brother-in-law."

"Dave O'Toole?"

"Yeah, your husband and Dave were in the Marines together."

"I'm sorry, but I don't know any Dave O'Toole."

"That's strange. You sent Dave and Colleen a card for Christmas just two months ago."

"What do you want, Mr. . . . ?"

"Regan. Tom Regan."

"What do you want, Mr. Regan?"

The lady frowned at Regan. He lowered his eyes to the pavement beneath his feet. He wondered why she was standing him off. He wondered why she was not telling him the truth. He raised his eyes to meet hers again as he decided to charge ahead.

"Look, Mrs. Bagdonovich, I'm a writer, and . . ."

"Not another one," she blurted out. "I'm sorry. I have nothing to say."

She started to close the door in Regan's face, but he pushed it open again and stepped inside the foyer. He closed the door after him.

"What do you think you're doing?" she demanded.

"I'm trying to get some answers."

"I told you that I have nothing to say. Now get out of my house."

She started to open the door again, but Regan leaned back against it.

"Look, Mrs. Bagdonovich, I want some straight answers, and after I get them, I'll leave."

"I'm going to call the police."

"No, you're not," said Regan. He felt she was bluffing.

She turned and walked into the living room. Regan followed her.

"Look, lady, I can see that you're afraid of something, but it shouldn't be me. I'm on your side. Dave O'Toole is my brother-in-law, and he told me all about your husband and him when they were in the Marines together. Now all I want to do is talk to your husband about some things that happened while they were in the Philippines."

"You can't do that," she said as she stopped reaching for the telephone.

"Why can't I?"

"Because my husband is dead!" she shrieked as she fell on the sofa crying.

Regan was dumbfounded. He did not know what to do next. There he was standing in the living room of a house that belonged to a lady that he had only met moments before, and she was lying on the sofa crying in front of him.

"Hey, get hold of yourself, will you?" he pleaded. "I didn't know he was dead."

"Well, now you do," she sobbed, "so get out."

The anguish in her voice matched the redness that surrounded her blue eyes. Her cheeks were smudged with mascara that had been washed there by her tears. She buried her face in the cushions again.

"I can only guess that your husband's death has something to do with what I came here to talk about. Is that it, Mrs. Bagdonovich? Because if it is, then you should know that I've come to help. Now won't you tell me about your husband's death?"

"I told you that I have nothing to say."

Regan was angered by her obstinate behavior. He bent over and grabbed her by her arms to straighten her upright.

"Don't touch me!" she screamed.

Regan shook her violently.

"Listen to me, lady," he growled. "If your husband's death was connected to the incidents in the Philippines, then that means that my sister and her husband are in danger. So am I, for that matter. If you want them on your conscience, then don't talk to me. But if you want to avenge your husband, then you'd better answer my questions, and you'd better answer them pretty damn quick."

Regan's face was only inches away from hers. The

terror that he had stricken her with was working. She stopped crying as her mind tried to cope with what he was telling her. They stared at each other. Anger flamed in his, and fear shadowed hers.

"All right," she whimpered. "What do you want to know?"

"Everything," he said as he released her from his grasp.

She reached for a tissue from a box on the end table. She wiped her nose and eyes as she composed herself.

"There isn't much to tell," she said softly.

"I'll be the judge of that," he snapped. "Hey, I'm sorry," he said as he realized that he might be frightening her even more.

She smiled at him, as if to forgive him without the use of words.

"Look, why don't we start all over?" said Regan as he pulled another tissue from the box and handed it to her. "You pull yourself together, and we'll talk this whole thing out. Okay?"

She shook her head in approval as she wiped her tear-stained cheeks.

"You missed some," said Regan as he took a third tissue and wiped away the last of the mascara.

"Thanks," she smiled again. "I'm sorry for behaving like such a fool."

"There's no need to apologize. I can't blame you."

"Well, what do you want to know first?"

"Well, I didn't know about your husband's death. Why don't you tell me about that first?"

"I'll start back when Paul got that phone call from the first writer. I suppose it all started with him.

"It was one night in December. Paul and I were home by ourselves as we usually were in the evening. The

29

phone rang and I answered. A man asked if he could speak to Paul. I asked who was calling and he said his name was Mr. Bertram. Paul came to the phone, and I went back to watching TV. When Paul was through talking about a half hour later, he came back in the living room and sat down next to me. I asked him who that Mr. Bertram was, and he said he was a writer. Before I could ask Paul anything else, he got up and went out on the patio. He seemed to be upset about the call. I followed him outside, and he told me about the call.

"He said that Mr. Bertram claimed to be a writer who was doing a book on the life of Lee Harvey Oswald. He had asked Paul if he could remember Oswald from his Marine Corps days, and Paul said he'd never forget the man that killed one of his best friends."

"Who was that?"

"Another Marine named Phil Schramm. Paul and your brother-in-law and Phil Schramm were really close in those days. Paul talked a lot about the three of them, but he had never told me that Lee Harvey Oswald had killed Schramm until the night that writer called.

"Well, this Mr. Bertram asked Paul if he could remember anything about Oswald, and Paul said all he knew about Oswald from those days was that Oswald was the guy who was supposed to relieve Schramm from guard duty the night he was killed. Other than that, Paul said he had never met Oswald. In fact, Paul had never even seen Oswald until after he killed President Kennedy and Paul saw him on TV. Paul said he was shocked because Oswald looked so much like his friend Schramm.

"Well, this Mr. Bertram seemed satisfied with that information, but he said he would be calling Paul again. He never called back.

"Two weeks later, Paul was killed in a car accident on the Black Canyon Highway; but in between those times, Paul told me he was worried about that Mr. Bertram calling him back. Paul had been thinking everything over, and he had come to some strange conclusions."

"Such as?"

"Well, the one he gave the most credibility to was that he felt that Oswald and Schramm were one and the same man. He said they looked enough alike to be twins."

"What else did Paul say about it?"

"He thought that if they were the same person, then Schramm didn't die that night in the Philippines. He just became Lee Harvey Oswald."

"Or he was Lee Harvey Oswald in the first place, and he was only masquerading as Schramm."

"Paul said the very same thing, but why would Oswald be Schramm?"

"Did Paul ever mention the U-2 flights or ever having seen a U-2 plane while he was in the Marines?"

"Now that you mention it, he did say that he and Dave wandered into a restricted area one day back in 1958. They both saw a U-2 plane in a hangar. That's all he ever said about it."

"What about your husband's accident? Do you think it was an accident?"

"The police said it was, but I think he was murdered."

"What makes you think that?"

"The Black Canyon Highway where Paul was killed is a four-lane, interstate highway. Paul's car had obviously been side-swiped and forced to crash into the mountainside. The police even admitted that it was a possibility, but they said it was highly unlikely.''

"Then you think Paul was killed because he knew something about Oswald and Schramm when they were in the service?''

"Yes, I do. I've been reading about some of the dissenting opinions on the Warren Commission findings, and I think Paul was one of the people who might have known one little fact that would cause Congress to keep on investigating President Kennedy's death.''

"What makes you so sure of that?''

"Two weeks ago, another man identifying himself as a writer, a Mr. Hewitt, called me, and he told me that.''

"A second writer told you that?''

"Yes, he said he was doing a book on Oswald's life, and he wanted to talk to Paul about it. After I told him that Paul was dead, he expressed his regrets; then he said, 'That's too bad, Mrs. Bagdonovich. You're late husband may have been the last connection between Schramm and Oswald. His testimony might make Congress sit up and take notice.' Those were his exact words to me. Then he said good-bye and hung up.''

"Have you told anyone else this?''

"No, just you.''

"Look, I think your life may be in danger, and now I know mine is. But I'm not worried about me. It's Dave and Colleen I'm worried about, and you, too. Fortunately, they had the foresight to keep their mouths shut about this, and you evidently know enough to not go blabbing it all over town.''

"I'd still like to find the people responsible for Paul's death.''

"So would I, but I want to explore this Oswald-Schramm connection a little further.''

Regan reached into his shirt pocked and removed the

photograph that he had taken from Colleen.

"Have you ever seen this person?" he asked when he presented the picture to Mrs. Bagdonovich.

"That's Lee Harvey Oswald, isn't it?"

"That's what I thought, too, but Dave says this is Phil Schramm."

Rita Bagdonovich wrinkled her brow in astonishment. Regan shook his head and chuckled lightly.

"The resemblance is remarkable," said Rita.

"I know. That's why I want to follow this thing through."

"Where are you going from here?"

"I suppose I should try to find out something about those writers who called here. One of them called Dave and Colleen in Tulsa. Did either of them say where they were from?"

"No, they only gave their names."

"That isn't much to go on, but I'll give it a shot."

"I'd like to help."

"You've been plenty of help already," said Regan as he rose to leave.

"But I want to do more."

"Well, if I need you for anything, I'll give you a call. Okay?"

"Okay."

Regan let himself out and returned to his motel to deliberate on the information that he had already learned. Something was still wrong with both his sister's and Rita Bagdonovich's stories. They just did not add up.

A writer by the name of Bertram calls Paul Bagdonovich in December; pumps him for information he knows about Schramm and Oswald; two weeks later, Bagdonovich is dead in an automobile accident that

Rita says is murder.

Rita receives a second call from a writer by the name of Hewitt; he doesn't know Paul is dead; and he tells Rita that Paul may have been the last link between Schramm and Oswald.

Colleen and Dave get a call from a writer whose name is . . . Is what? What was that writer's name?''

Regan picked up his telephone and placed a call to Colleen in Tulsa.

"Hello, Colleen? This is Tom."

"Hi, Tommy. What did Paul Bagdonovich tell you?"

"He didn't tell me a thing. He's dead."

"He's dead?"

"Yes, he's dead, but never mind that now. I can't afford to make this a long conversation. Just answer a few questions for me. What was the name of that writer who called Dave?"

"Um'm, Hughes or Hewler or something like that."

"Was it Hewitt?"

"That sounds like it. Why?"

"Never mind. Did he say where he was from?"

"I think he did. I think he said he was from Salt Lake City. Why? What's this all about?"

"Colleen, will you let me ask the questions?"

"Sorry."

"That's better. Now didn't you tell me that he had told you that he had spoken with Paul Bagdonovich?"

"Yes, he said that Paul had told him that part about Oswald relieving Schramm on guard duty the night Schramm was killed. Why all these questions?"

"I told you never mind. I'll tell you about it some other time when I can afford to talk longer. Thanks for the information. I'll call you when I get to Salt Lake."

Providing I get the dough to go to Salt Lake, said

34

Regan to himself.

Regan decided to take the bull by the horns. He was in need of money to complete the research he had begun. Since he was a writer with some ability, he decided the best place to obtain that money would be at a newspaper. He would try to get an advance on the story that he was certain he would eventually write about Oswald. He was certain that a story existed. Why else would two other writers, if they were writers, be trying to glean information about an incident that had happened eighteen years before?

The Morning Sun was the leading newspaper in the Southwest, and it was located right there in Phoenix. Regan decided to start at the top and work down. That was why he was in the office of Milton Harris, the managing editor of THE SUN promptly at eight o'clock that Monday morning.

Regan did not wait for the secretary to let him into the editor's office. He simply walked in and made himself comfortable, which was not easy, considering the condition of the office. It was something out of an old Bogart movie. Venetian blinds still covered the windows. The carpeting on the floor had seen its best days. The paint was peeling off the ceiling, and cracks were quite visible in the plaster walls. The furniture would have looked better in the showroom of an antique shop. An old wooden desk dominated the room. Behind it was an equally old wooden swivel chair. Two metal but padded armchairs faced the front of the desk. From the looks of the office, Regan was beginning to think he was Clark Kent and Perry White would come walking in any second.

Regan was sitting on the edge of the desk when the middle-aged Harris walked in. Harris glanced at him, then looked at the name on the door. The balding and gray-templed editor raised his eyebrows, bent his head to one side, then closed the door behind him. He carried his coat over his arm and a briefcase in the hand of the same arm. He took the last two steps up to Regan, staring the young writer directly in the eye.

"Pardon me," said Harris, "you must be the new boss around here."

Regan did not budge.

"I used to be," Harris continued, "but I never let anyone plant his ass on my desk like that."

Regan could see what he was getting at, but he remained seated.

"Well, since you're sitting there, it must be your desk now. Right?"

"Well, no," stammered Regan.

"Then it must still be mine. In that case, you'd better get your ass off it and pretty damn quick!"

Regan hopped to his feet at the intonation of the command. His toes danced nervously inside his shoes as he watched the editor walked around behind his desk.

"Are you still here?" asked Harris as he set his briefcase down on the desk.

"Yes, sir," replied Regan meekly.

"Why?" asked Harris simply.

"Well, I'm here to see you, Mr. Harris," said the quivering writer.

Harris hooked his coat on the hat tree behind the desk.

"Who are you and what are you doing in my office?"

"The name is Tom Regan, and I'm here to make you an offer."

"Sorry, I'm not in the market right now, so get out of

here. I have work to do."

"Not till you hear me out."

Harris squatted gently into his chair, pulled himself up to the desk, then reached for the telephone. Regan's hand shot out from his body, as if he was going to prevent Harris from using the device to summon some assistant. Harris gave the hand an icy stare, and it retreated to its previous position.

"Give me a chance, will you?" pleaded Regan.

Harris ignored the anguish in the young man's voice as he dialed the four numbers that would connect him with the security office.

"Hello, security? This is Milt Harris. I've got a pest in my office that I want removed immediately."

Regan was not going to give up yet.

"That should give me a minute or two to tell you what I've got."

"I hope it's not contagious," said Harris as he replaced the receiver.

"It might be," retorted Regan. "You won't know if you don't hear me out."

There was an urgency in the bearded intruder's tone that touched Harris.

"All right then, you've got sixty seconds," he said as he checked his watch. "Go. "

"I have reason to believe that Lee Harvey Oswald was an agent for our government."

"Not that crap again. That's already been done a few million times."

Regan reached into his pocket and removed the same photograph that he had shown to Rita Bagdonovich. He handed it over to Harris.

"Do you recognize the man in that picture?"

"Sure," said Harris after careful consideration. "It's

37

Lee Harvey Oswald.''

"Wrong!" said an elated Regan. "It's Phil Schramm, a fellow Marine that Oswald may have murdered in 1959 at Cubi Point, The Philippines.''

The editor's head bobbed up to see the smile on Regan's face, and then he returned his attention to the photograph.

"What are you talking about?" asked Harris.

"It's a long story," said Regan as he realized that he had Harris hooked.

There was a knock at the door.

"Come in," said Harris.

It was the security guard.

"Is this the pest, Mr. Harris?" the blue uniformed officer asked as he eyed Regan.

"I'm not so sure, Hank. You'd better wait outside for a minute. I'll call you if I need you.''

The guard nodded and stepped back through the doorway, closing the door behind him.

"So let's hear your story," said Harris as he leaned back in his chair.

Regan went on to relate everything he knew up to that point in his investigation. He took nearly ten minutes to finish his tale.

"Is that it?" asked Harris.

"That's it so far. I know there could be more if only I had the money to carry out my investigation.''

"Now I get it," sneered Harris. "You really had me going there for a moment, but it won't work. You aren't going to con me out of a dime.''

"I'm not trying to con anyone out of anything," snapped Regan right back at Harris. "I've got a story here; a fantastic story. There might be a lot more here than meets the eye, but I need the backing to find out.''

"Well, you'll have to look elsewhere."

"Look, Mr. Harris, I quit my job to pursue this. I believe there's something in all this that might lead me to the solving of President Kennedy's assassination."

"What makes you think that?"

"I've done a lot of studying on the assassination and on Oswald. Do you remember anything about the Warren Commission testimony of Oswald's mother?"

"No, why?"

"Oswald's mother kept insisting that Oswald was an agent of some kind, but she didn't know who for. Now just supposing that Schramm and Oswald were the same person, then it would mean that Oswald was an agent in disguise as Schramm. That would explain why the Marines have no record of Schramm."

"Why would the Marines have a spy in their own ranks?"

"Who knows? Maybe he wasn't working for the Marines. Maybe he was working for the CIA. My brother-in-law and Paul Bagdonovich were air-traffic controllers when they were in the Marines. They were at one of the bases in Japan where the U-2 flights originated, and the CIA was in charge of those operations. The CIA could have had Oswald watching them to make certain they weren't selling any secrets to the Russians about the U-2 planes or the flights."

"Okay, Oswald was an agent. So what?"

"So maybe I can prove it."

"And?"

"If I can prove that, then I can prove that some of those claims that he was an agent, that he was working for the CIA or the FBI, and that he was framed are all true and not a lot of speculative hogwash."

"You might be right. You've certainly raised some

very interesting points. I'd like to see this thing to the end myself. Do you think you can do it?''

"I know I can if I have the financial backing to pursue this lead to the end.''

Harris studied his visitor intently. He was searching his soul as well as Regan's. He frowned first, then shook his head to clear it.

"I don't usually play hunches,'' said Harris, "but this one is too strong to pass up.''

Harris reached inside his coat to remove his wallet. From the billfold, he took out five twenty dollar bills and three credit cards. He placed the bills and cards in front of Regan.

"There is no way,'' said Harris, "that I could get a project like this okayed by my superiors; so I guess I'll have to back you myself. All I want is for you to keep me posted on whatever you're doing and wherever you are. As you get information, I want it sent here, to me, immediately. If you ever make me think that you're trying to screw me, I'll have you in jail in twenty-four hours. Do I make myself perfectly clear?''

"Yes, sir,'' replied Regan, even though his eyes were still fixed to the money and the credit cards, "but how are you going to get your money back?''

"If you have a story here, the paper will pay me for whatever it cost. If you haven't got a story, then you're going to have to figure out a way to pay me back. Is that understood?''

"Perfectly,'' said Regan as he picked up the money and the credit cards. "I'll call you from Salt Lake.''

"Not so fast,'' said Harris. "Hank, come in here.''

"Yes, Mr. Harris?'' said the guard as he entered the office.

"Take this young man down to personnel and make

certain that he fills out an application to work here. Check his driver's license to make sure he puts the right name on the application. As soon as he's done, let him go and bring his application back up here to me.''

''Yes, sir.''

''Hold it. I don't live here. What do I put down for an address?''

Harris scribbled his address on a piece of paper and handed it to Regan.

''That's mine,'' said Harris. ''It'll do till you get back. Besides, that way your paychecks will be sent to me. A little insurance never hurt anyone.''

''The name is Regan, Thomas Marshall Regan; but I'd like my byline to read, 'by Regan.' That'll be sufficient from now on.''

Harris frowned as he pointed at the door. Regan and the guard got the idea without further elaboration.

V

Salt Lake City

February 16-17, 1977

Regan was in the office of Wendell Preston, the managing editor of *The Salt Lake City Chronicle*. He sat patiently in an armchair as he waited for Preston to conclude his telephone conversation. He relaxed in the luxurious surroundings of the room, which appeared to be more a suite than an office.

Indirect lighting illuminated everything in such a way that there were no shadows to be seen. The leather upholstered furniture would have fit perfectly in any modern living room. Only the antique desk gave any semblance to the room being an office. Even the deep purple carpet seemed to be out of place. Regan was deeply impressed, but he was more impressed by the man speaking on the telephone.

Wendell Preston was nearly the same age as his counterpart in Phoenix, but his appearance was that of a much younger man. His dark brown hair was barely gray at the temples. The crow's feet at the corners of his eyes were barely noticeable. The skin of his neck had not yet begun to sag. He wore a sportcoat that also hid his true age. The bright blue in the coat accentuated Preston's eyes.

Regan felt a little shabby in comparison. His pale green coat had long ago lost its newness, and his striped tie was displaying a few frayed threads. His shoes had not been polished in a month, and the scuff marks on their black leather stood out like so many scars. At least they were comfortable.

Preston finished his call and turned his attention to the bearded young man sitting across the desk from him. He smiled politely, almost in toleration.

"Now, Mr. Regan, what were you saying?"

"I was about to ask you if you had ever heard of a writer by the name of Hewitt."

"Hewitt? Hewitt?" said Preston pensively. "That name does seem to strike a familiar note. Do you have a first name?"

"No, I don't. All I know about him is that he lives here in Salt Lake or in the vicinity."

"Well, if he's a known writer, then we should have some reference to him in our files."

Preston depressed the intercom button on his office control panel.

"Miss Snow, would you come in here please?"

"Yes, sir," came the reply.

The secretary glided into the room and up to the left end of Preston's desk. She stood erect in near perfect posture, almost as if she was standing at attention in a military parade.

"Miss Snow, I'd like you to meet Mr. Regan," said Preston.

The secretary and Regan exchanged nods as they acknowledged the introduction.

"I'd like you to take Mr. Regan down to our records department. Introduce him to our files of microfilm, and show him how to use the viewer."

"Yes, sir."

"I think you'll find your Mr. Hewitt down there, Mr. Regan."

"I certainly hope so," said Regan.

The two men shook hands, and Regan followed Miss Snow into the outer office on their way to the records department.

It took Regan nearly an hour before he found the man he was certain was the Hewitt that had called both his brother-in-law and Rita Bagdonovich. The article on the viewer screen was from the society page. It listed a writer by the name of Caleb J. Hewitt from Murray, Utah being a guest at a party. Regan made a note of the town and the name before going on to the next article with the name Hewitt in it.

Two articles later Regan found a book review that listed Caleb J. Hewitt as the author of a non-fiction work on the history of Utah. That just about sealed it as far as Regan was concerned, but he continued to look for additional information. None was to be found in the remaining four articles.

After leaving *The Chronicle*, Regan went to a telephone booth to look up Caleb J. Hewitt in the white pages of the directory. He found him and his address in Murray, which was a suburb of Salt Lake City. Caleb J. Hewitt lived on a numbered street, which made it easy for Regan to find the house.

A few sharp raps on the door were answered by a woman in her late thirties. She gave Regan a polite smile that highlighted the rosiness of her cheeks. The glow in her blue eyes made Regan feel welcome, as did the softness in her voice.

"Hello, may I help you?" she asked.

"Yes, I'm looking for Caleb Hewitt," said Regan.

"He's busy right now, but if you'll give me your name, I'll ask if he can see you." She stepped back. "Won't you come in?"

44

"Thank you," said Regan as he stepped inside. "My name is Tom Regan. I'm a writer with *The Morning Sun* in Phoenix."

"If you'll wait here, Mr. Regan, I'll check with my husband."

Mrs. Hewitt went down a short hall and turned to the right. Less than a minute passed, and she reappeared from the same place. She was followed by an obese man wearing metal-rimmed glasses. The lady stepped aside to permit him to pass. He waddled down the hall toward Regan extending a pudgy hand out of a long sleeve shirt.

"Mr. Regan, I'm delighted to meet you," he said in a high-pitched nasal twang. "I'm Cal Hewitt, and what can I do for you?"

"I'm with *The Morning Sun* in Phoenix," said Regan.

"Yes, my wife told me."

"I'm also Dave O'Toole's brother-in-law."

"Dave O'Toole?"

"In Tulsa?"

"Oh, yes, that Dave O'Toole. The ex-Marine I called about the Oswald book. Yes, I remember now. He wasn't much help to me."

"Well, maybe I'll make up for it," volunteered Regan. "And maybe you can help me."

"Oh? How so?"

"Why don't you take Mr. Regan into your study, dear?" interrupted his wife. "You can be more comfortable in there."

"Yes, let's go in here where we can sit down for a nice talk," offered Hewitt as he retreated toward the doorway that he had just come from.

Regan took the few steps to the study entering the cluttered room by edging past the rotund Hewitt. He hesitated to sit down because the sofa was strewn with sheets of typing paper, books, and pamphlets. Only the chair in front of the desk where Hewitt obviously was going to sit was free from debris.

"Oh, please excuse the mess," said Hewitt as he bustled past Regan to clear a place for the visitor to sit on the sofa. "I'm not a very neat person in this room. My wife detests coming in here. I won't let her touch anything in here. This is my domain, and the rest of the house is her responsibility. There you go."

Regan seated himself in the space that Hewitt had made for him. Hewitt floundered backwards to his chair. He steadied himself against the back of it before easing himself down on the seat.

"There," heaved Hewitt, as he was quite out of breath from the minor exertion. "Now how can we help each other?"

Regan reached into his inside coat pocket to retrieve the picture of Phil Schramm. He handed it to Hewitt as both men stretched to make the exchange.

"Have you ever seen that man?" asked Regan.

Hewitt smiled with angelic delight.

"Why, this is Lee Harvey Oswald," said Hewitt, as if he was a child in a classroom answering his teacher correctly. He returned the photograph.

"Not according to my brother-in-law," Regan contradicted. "He claims that man is Phil Schramm, a fellow Marine who was supposed to have committed suicide at Cubi Point in 1959."

"Oh, really? But who is this Schramm fellow?"

"You mean you don't know?"

"No, I'm sorry, but I've never heard of him. Who is he?"

"You mean you didn't tell Rita Bagdonovich that her husband may have been the last link between Oswald

46

and Schramm?''

"I'm sorry again, Mr. Regan. Once more you have the better of me. Who is Rita Bag-whatever?''

Regan was incredulous. He had expected Hewitt to fill in a number of missing pieces to the puzzle that he had discovered, but Hewitt was acting totally ignorant of the subject at hand.

"Mr. Hewitt, we'd better start from the beginning. You are doing a book on the life of Lee Harvey Oswald, are you not?''

"Why, yes, I am.''

"You did speak with Dave O'Toole on the night of February, uh, seventh, didn't you?''

"I can't say for certain what the date was. I'll have to check my notes. Pardon me.''

Hewitt turned around in the chair and rifled through some of the papers on his desk. He muttered to himself under his breath as he did. He found the one he was searching for, then turned his attention back to Regan.

"Here it is,'' said Hewitt as he held up the paper for Regan to see. "Now let me see. O'Toole, O'Toole. Ah, yes, here he is. Yes, I did speak with Mr. O'Toole on the night of February seventh.''

"And didn't you try to get in touch with Paul Bagdonovich in Phoenix about two weeks ago?''

"Could you spell that last name for me, please?''

Regan spelled it.

"Oh, Bagdonovich,'' said Hewitt, as if he recognized the name for the first time. "Let me see. Bagdonovich. Here he is. No, no, I've made no attempt to contact Mr. Bagdonovich yet.''

"You haven't?''

"No, not yet, but if you think I should. . . .''

"No, it wouldn't do you any good. He's dead.''

47

"Oh, that is too bad. How did he die?"

"Car accident last December."

"Such a pity," clucked Hewitt.

"Mr. Hewitt, who knows about this book that you're writing on Oswald?"

"There must be dozens of people. Why?"

"Because someone is calling people on that list of yours saying that they are you."

"Why would anyone want to do that?"

"Good question," remarked Regan. "A better one is, who knows about that list you have there?"

"That does narrow things down a bit," smiled Hewitt. "Besides myself, there is my wife and my three research assistants.

"What research assistants?" asked Regan as he removed his notebook from his shirt pocket.

"Well, I employ three young ladies to do the research for my books. There's Angela Hargrove who lives in Bountiful; Valerie Davis who lives in Salt Lake City; and Sheile Simmons who also lives in Salt Lake City."

"Why do these three ladies have that list?"

"Actually, each one only has a third of the list. They locate the present whereabouts of the people on the list. They do the leg work of finding them, and then I contact them directly, just as I did in the case of your brother-in-law. They start at the place that the person was last known to reside or with a relative who might know where they are now, and then my researchers go from there."

"Do you have a listing of who has which third of the list?"

"I believe so," said Hewitt as he turned to rifle through the mess on his desk again. "Yes, here they are." He held them up for Regan to see.

"Are Dave and Paul Bagdonovich on the same list?"

"Let me see," said Hewitt as he shuffled the three sheets of paper in search of the two names. "Yes, here they are. Valerie Davis has that third. Both names are on her list."

"You said she lives in Salt Lake," said Regan as he checked his notes. "Could I have her address?"

Hewitt wrote her address on the back of her list of names and presented the sheet to Regan.

"Thank you very much, Mr. Hewitt," said Regan as he came to his feet to leave.

"You're very welcome, Mr. Regan, but I thought you had some information for me as well."

"Sorry, I almost forgot," said Regan as he sat down again.

Regan began by telling Hewitt about the man in the photograph that he had shown him and his connection with Oswald, Bagdonovich, and Dave O'Toole. Hewitt seemed to be quite impressed with the story.

"This may prove that Oswald was with the CIA way back then," said Regan. "All we have to do is find someone who was there at the time of Schramm's death and who will testify to the fact that it happened and to the circumstances surrounding the event. If we can find that person, then he could lead us to others who will also testify about it. That should lead us to the link between Oswald and the CIA. That's what I'm trying to do with my investigation."

"And a very important investigation it is, Mr. Regan. I should like very much to know the results when you are finished."

"You got a deal, Mr. Hewitt. You'll get a copy of my story the same day my editor does."

"That would be very nice of you."

"Think nothing of it," said Regan as he once more stood to leave.

Hewitt labored to his feet and offered to shake hands with Regan. He accepted, and Hewitt followed him to the door. They bade each other farewell and good luck as Regan departed.

Regan noted that Valerie Davis resided in apartment number thirteen of the Foothill Arms ten blocks north of the capitol district of Salt Lake City. He had little trouble finding the address. He parked across the street from the two-story building that has outdoor entrances for each apartment. He stopped at the mail boxes near the entrance to the building to make certain that Valerie lived in number thirteen. The address was correct, but he discovered a second name, C. Perkins, written under hers on the nameplate She evidently had a roommate. He hoped to find one of them home that afternoon.

Number thirteen was upstairs toward the back. He rang the doorbell and waited with his back to the door. When he heard the door being opened, he turned around to see a blue-eyed brunette smiling at him.

"Hi! Can I do something for you?" she drawled.

"You're already doing it," smiled Regan.

"I'm glad to hear it," she said as she leaned against the door frame. "Did you want something in particular?"

"Yeah, but business comes first."

"I hope you're not going to try to sell me something I don't need."

"No, I'm looking for Valerie Davis."

"That's worse. I think I'd rather have you be a salesman."

"Then you're not Valerie Davis?"

"No, I'm Cindy Perkins. Valerie's still at work. She

won't be home for at least two hours.''

''I was afraid of that.''

''Don't be so disappointed. I'm not exactly what you're looking for, but I do have my good points.''

''Yes, I can see that, but I still have to talk to Miss Davis.''

''Well, Valerie and I are pretty close. Maybe I might know what you want to find out from her. Why don't you come in and talk to me?''

''Why not? I haven't got anything better to do for the next few hours.''

As Regan stepped through the doorway past her, he took a better look at Cindy. She had an average figure, not too many curves, and she was slightly overweight. Her breasts were what a more licentious man would call ''bite-size,'' and her hips filled her bluejeans to the seams. The perfume she was wearing was having its intended effect on Regan.

''I've told you my name,'' she said. ''Why don't you tell me yours?''

''It's Regan. Tom Regan.'' He reached for his wallet. ''I'm with *The Morning Sun* in Phoenix.'' He showed her his press card.

''Oh, you're a reporter,'' she said, smiling.

''No, I like to think of myself as a writer,'' he said as he replaced his wallet and sat down on the sofa. ''Right now I'm doing a story on Lee Harvey Oswald, and I wanted to talk to Miss Davis about her role as a researcher for Caleb Hewitt.''

''Oh, yeah,'' she said as she sat down next to him. ''She's been doing that research stuff for him for quite a while now. Valerie says it's really a lot of fun to trace all those people for Hewy-baby. She gets a real kick out of it.''

51

"Then you're familiar with her work?"

"No, not really. I just know that she spends a lot of time on the phone and she writes a lot of letters. It's a good thing Hewy-baby pays the tab for all that."

"Runs up a big bill with the telephone company, I suppose."

"You bet she does, and stamps and stationery don't come cheap either. Last month's bills for that came to over thirty dollars, and the phone bill was over two hundred."

"And Hewitt pays for all of it?"

"Like clockwork. She gets the bill, takes it over to him, and he writes her a check for the full amount. That fat, little lecher must be loaded."

"What makes you think that?"

"Valerie took one of his checks to his bank to cash once. You know, to make sure it was good. It was a big check for over six big ones. The teller took one look at the name on the check and forked over the bread just like that. She didn't even bother to see if he had that much in his account. From the house he lives in, you'd never guess he had that kind of money."

"You called him a lecher. Why?"

"Because the little creep tried something with me. that's why."

I can't blame him, thought Regan.

"Has he tried anything with Miss Davis?"

"He wouldn't dare. Her ex-husband would tear him apart if he tried."

"Ex-husband?"

"Yeah, Valerie was married to this creepy Texan for a few years. He drank like a sailor, swore like one, and chased other women like the whole fleet. He's even tried getting it on with me, but I'm too good a friend of

52

Valerie's to ever let that happen. Even though they're divorced, he's still not my style. Say, could I fix you a drink or offer you a cold beer while we wait for Valerie?"

"Sure. What have you got?"

"You name it."

"You sound like a regular bartender."

"I am. I work down at the Pink Lady, but this is my night off."

"Well, in that case, I'll have a whiskey sour."

"Coming right up," said Cindy as she headed for the refrigerator.

Regan leaned back on the sofa to observe his surroundings. From what he could see, the apartment was obviously very small; probably two bedrooms, a kitchen, living room, and a bath. They were probably all painted in FHA-VA white. The tan carpet was well-worn in the travel areas, which suggested that it had barely met the government's requirements when it was installed. The furniture was modern American cheap, which told him that the women residing there had not purchased it. The off-white drapes also suggested the taste of federal inspectors. The residents had made an effort to adorn the room with their own touch by hanging pictures and a tapestry. A few weird ashtrays were placed about the room in a further attempt to improve the class of the flat.

Cindy returned with his drink in a regular bar room glass. Regan did not have to ask how she had acquired it. She also had a drink as she relaxed on the sofa within inches of him.

"Let's not talk about Hewy-baby or Valerie anymore," she said. "Why don't you tell me about Tom Regan?"

Her interest in him was flattering. Regan could see through it, but he loved it.

An hour and four drinks later, Regan found himself in the not so untenable position of complete nakedness in Cindy's bed. They loved, and both of them loved it. Only the sound of Valerie's voice in the living room discontinued their concerto in sex. Cindy threw on a bathrobe and went out to greet her roommate as Regan dressed.

When he emerged from the bedroom, Regan was greeted by the striking beauty of Valerie Davis. Her brassy hair was in the latest Hollywood sex-symbol style. Her blue eyes did not have the same allure as her well-designed body. They were almost sad but sincerely friendly, as was her smile when she approached him.

"Hi, I'm Valerie Davis," she said as she extended her hand to him.

"I'm glad to meet you," responded Regan as he caught his breath and shook her hand.

"Cindy tells me you're a newspaperman with a paper in Phoenix and that you're doing a story on Oswald like Cal Hewitt."

"That's right, I am. I wanted to talk to you about your part as Mr. Hewitt's research assistant."

"Well, I don't do all that much."

"Don't let her kid you, Tom," said Cindy as she headed for the bedroom to dress. "She does plenty."

"Why don't we sit down, Mr. Regan?"

He accepted her invitation by relaxing on the sofa. Valerie seated herself in the only armchair in the room.

"Now," she sighed, "how can I help you?"

"You can start by telling me how you go about locating all these people for Cal Hewitt. You know, like where do you start? What methods do you use? Does anyone help you?"

"In the first place, I do it all myself," she said defensively. From there, she gave him a detailed account of how she went about tracing people. She offered him no clues about who might be calling the same people and impersonating Caleb Hewitt.

"That's really interesting, Mrs. Davis," said Regan.

"Please call me Valerie. I hate being referred to as Mrs. Davis."

"Okay, Valerie. Would you mind telling me a few things about yourself? Where you were born; where you were raised; the college you went to; what started you in this business; your ambitions. Stuff like that."

"Why would you be interested in me?"

"Human interest stuff. People always want to read about other people and what they're doing and how they got there."

"Okay, but there isn't much to tell."

Born Valerie Victoria Edwards in Dallas, Texas, she did not grow up there, which explained the absence of an accent in her speech. Her father had been on the faculty of Bishop College in Dallas, but the family had moved to Salt Lake City when she was two years old because her father had accepted a position at the University of Utah. After graduating from high school in 1967, she had returned to Dallas to attend Bishop College, where she had met William Davis who was also attending classes there. They had married after her graduation in 1971. The couple had then moved to Phoenix in 1972, but their marriage had lasted only three years before Valerie sued for divorce on the grounds of incompatibility. Davis had fought the legal proceeding and appeared to be winning until he went into one of his many tirades in the courtroom. His outburst had cost him thirty days in jail and his wife.

Valerie had moved to Salt Lake City in order to get away from Davis, but he had found out where she had gone and had followed her. Claiming that he was a changed man, Davis visited her occasionally although Valerie would never stay in the same room with him without Cindy being there.

She had begun working for Hewitt the previous autumn in order to supplement her income from her full-time job as a corporate secretary. The work for Hewitt was very enjoyable and interesting, but she did not particularly care for Hewitt.

"I'm not sure why I don't like him," said Valerie. "He's never done anything offensive to me, but there's just something about him that gives me the creeps. It's as though he isn't what he seems to be."

"That's strange," said Regan. "I got the same feeling when I talked with him this afternoon."

"I'll tell you what it is," said Cindy as she came out of the bedroom. "He's a lecherous little creep who can't keep his hands to himself."

"Cool it, Cindy," warned Valerie. "It's more than that. It's as if he had something to hide. I don't know what it could be, and I don't really care as long as he keeps the money coming my way."

"Valerie, does anyone other than Cindy, Hewitt, and you know about the work you're doing for him? I mean the specific kind of work you're doing."

"Not that I know of," said Valerie. "I don't talk about it because Hewitt warned me that it might be dangerous if I did. He nearly scared the hell out of me when he told me that."

"Did he say why it might be dangerous?"

56

"He told me how a lot of people who had been witnesses to the Kennedy assassination had died in a lot of mysterious ways. He said that even some writers had either died or had their lives threatened for digging too deep into Oswald's life."

"He wasn't wrong about that," conceded Regan. "There have been a lot of strange deaths connected to Oswald or the assassination."

"Stop it, Tom," said Cindy. "Valerie's already scared enough."

"It's okay, Cindy," said Valerie.

"Well, you've been a lot of help, Valerie," said Regan as he stood up. "I want to thank you for your co-operation. This should add a great deal to my story."

"You're not going, are you?" Cindy said, pouting.

"Sorry, Babe, but I have to," said Regan as he moved toward the door. "I've got to work up my notes from today."

"You won't be working on them all night, will you?"

"I could be persuaded to take a break a little later this evening," said Regan at the door.

"Where are you staying?" she asked.

"I'm at the Capitol Motel on South State, room number eight. I'll be taking a break around nine."

"I just might drop by."

Regan opened the door and stepped outside. Out of the corner of his eye he caught the image of a man coming his way.

"I'll be looking forward to it," said Regan, just before leaning inside to kiss her good-bye.

Cindy blew him another kiss as he stepped back on the balcony. She closed the door as he turned away from it.

Regan took two steps toward the stairs before looking

up to see a taller man with a black mustache approaching him along the balcony. The man smiled savagely, before throwing his big right fist toward Regan's face. The punch sent Regan reeling backward, his hands groping for anything to help him stay on his feet. His left hand grabbed the railing of the balcony, and his back crashed into an iron roof support pole. The collision shook the balcony.

Regan was stunned but still alert enough to duck out of the way of the next blow from the dark stranger. He lunged a shoulder into the man's midsection, which drove him back against the wall. Even with the wind knocked out of him, the bigger man had the strength to bring his clasped hands down hard on Regan's back between the shoulder blades. Regan's knees wobbled before giving way. He fell to the walkway rolling away as soon as he hit. Good that he did, because a black cowboy boot sailed past his head and crashed into the wall.

The door to number thirteen flew open. Valerie and Cindy moved quickly between Regan and his attacker. Regan tasted the blood in his mouth as he saw the two girls through blurred vision as they forced the dark stranger away from him.

"What are you doing, Bill?" screamed Valerie.

That was the last sound to penetrate Regan's brain as he crossed over into unconsciousness.

His first reaction when awakened minutes later on the sofa in the girls' apartment was almost expected. He reached for his painful mouth, wondering what had caused the damage. Then he remembered, and his anger at being assaulted revived him completely.

"Who the hell hit me?" he demanded. His lips were already beginning to swell.

"Valerie's ex-husband," said Cindy as she held out a washcloth wrapped around two ice cubes.

Regan allowed her to place the cold compress on his mouth.

"I told you he was an animal," said Cindy. "He thought you were here seeing Valerie for other reasons. He thought you were kissing her good-bye instead of me."

"Where is he now?" asked Regan as he pushed Cindy's hand away.

"Valerie got him out of here before one of the neighbors called the cops. Damn that sonofabitch! He's caused her more trouble than I want to remember."

Regan started to sit up, but the pain between his shoulder blades prevented him from rising more than half upright. He fell back against the cushions. He winced with the additional pain.

"Take it easy, lover. Big Bill worked you over pretty bad. He used to box in the Marines. Valerie said he beat up every man he fought."

"I can believe it," said Regan. "I feel like I've been mangled by one of the best."

"Well, he's gone now, so you just lay there and take it easy. Do you want me to fix you a drink?"

"Sure. Maybe it'll kill the pain."

Two drinks later, Regan had recovered sufficiently enough to drive himself back to his motel. Cindy followed him in her car. Inside his room, she aided him in undressing. She removed her own clothes, and they stood naked, facing each other.

"I know what you want," said Regan, "but I don't think I'm up to it."

"That's okay, Tom," said Cindy as she nudged him toward the bed. "You just relax, and I'.. give you a back rub."

Regan did as he was told, and Cindy massaged him to sleep. Not wishing to drive home at such a late hour, she pulled the covers over them and stayed the night. Regan was in better condition to make use of her company in the morning.

"What's next on the agenda?" asked Cindy as she dressed.

"I'm not sure yet," said Regan, lying. "I suppose I'll go back to Phoenix to write this story."

"Will you be coming back to Salt Lake soon?"

"I certainly hope so. It seems friendly enough around here."

"In spite of what happened last night?"

"If you're referring to the beating I took, the answer is yes. If you're referring to everything else, then the answer is no."

Cindy liked that answer and let Regan know it by embracing him. Regan was beginning to like this girl for more than physical reasons.

"There's still three hours before check out time," said Regan as he smiled at her affectionately. "Why don't we go have some breakfast?"

"My stomach thought you'd never ask."

As Cindy ate, Regan sipped coffee through his swollen lips. Their conversation was irrelevant to what Regan was really thinking. He was planning his next step for finding Phil Schramm.

While Cindy had been in the shower, Regan had gone over the list of names that Cal Hewitt had given him. One name in particular stuck out in his mind. It was the initials after the name that captured his attention. The name was Robert Delano Crowell, but the letters "Lt.

60

USMC OOD CB, P'' were printed after it. Regan could not understand why Hewitt had made a note after Crowell's name. He deciphered the initials to mean, "Lieutenant United States Marine Corps Officer of the Day Cubi Point, Philippines." He wondered why Hewitt would be interested in the OOD at Cubi Point. He would have to talk to Crowell to find that out.

"Would you like to see some of the sights of the city?" asked Cindy when she finished her meal.

The question startled Regan out of thinking about his next step.

"Actually, I had another thought in mind," he said. "Some indoor activity would be more to my liking."

"That sounds interesting enough to me," she smiled. "I'm more of an indoor person myself."

"Then what are we waiting for?"

They returned to Regan's motel room where they had a long farewell. An hour after their last kiss, Regan was driving along Interstate 80 for Portland to find Robert Delano Crowell.

VI

Oregon

February 18–19, 1977

Interstate 80-North was uncompleted around Caldwell, Idaho. Travellers still had to drive through the town, which made it an ideal place for hitchhikers to find a ride.

That was why Regan was slowing his Toyota to forty-five miles per hour. He was hoping to see someone thumbing a ride in the direction he was going. The trip from Salt Lake City to Portland was over seven hundred miles and, although Regan had not yet seen that part of the country, also very boring like most trips taken over interstate highways. Regan only wanted to help someone reach his destination and at the same time provide him with a little conversation.

Luck was with Regan. Up ahead on the side of the road he saw a person sitting on some baggage. As he closed in on the pedestrian, he could see that it was a man, probably a college student, wearing a green fatigue jacket. The baggage was a backpack and sleeping bag. The young man had long brown hair that covered his ears. He did not look up immediately when Regan stopped his car a few lengths beyond the hitchhiker. Regan tapped his horn once, and the young man was in motion picking up his gear and running toward the car.

Regan reached over to unlock the doors on the passenger side. The young man opened the back door to put his gear on the back seat. He closed the door and climbed into the front seat. Both men eyed each other warily as hitchhikers and lone drivers do upon first meeting. Hitchhikers were always on the alert for homosexuals, and lone drivers worried themselves with questions about the rider's background. There was no telling which one might be a thief or a murderer. Those thoughts raced through the minds of both men as Regan put the car in gear and steered back into the traffic.

"Where you headed?" asked Regan.

"L.A.," said the rider.

"Isn't this the long way around?"

"Yeah, but it's easier to get a ride this way than it is going through Salt Lake. It's also easier to get a ride out of Portland."

"I can dig it," said Regan in an attempt to let the young man know that he was cool. "Well, you're in luck because I'm going to Portland. I don't know how much that's going to help, because we won't get there till late tonight. It's a bad scene to get stuck in a big city late at night. That happened to me a few times when I was hitchhiking my way around the country."

"Are you a reporter?"

Regan was caught off guard. Taken aback at first, he then realized that he still had his Wisconsin press sticker on the front windshield.

"Oh, you mean the sticker on the window," said Regan. "I work for *The Morning Sun* in Phoenix. I'm not really a reporter. I like to think of myself as a writer of news, sort of a feature-story writer."

From there, Regan told the young man a few minor details about his job, and the rider opened up with similar details about himself. His name was Mike Pearson from Downey, California. He was only eighteen but already on his own. Mike had been living in Boise with a twenty-six year old divorcée. He had tired of living with the same woman, so he had decided to return to California where he could find a job and another woman, preferably one without children.

Their conversation took a more ribald turn at that point as Mike related some intimate details of his recent relationship. Not to be outdone by a mere youth, Regan countered with tales of his sexual exploits as both a teenager and an adult. He mentioned long love affairs as well as one-night stands with lonely woman who only wanted to sleep with a man. His favorite story was about the woman who had lived next door when he was in high school in California. He was in the midst of telling Mike how she had initiated him into her neighborhood sex club when he spotted a road sign that advised that a rest area was two miles ahead. He continued with that story until he eased the car off the highway onto the exit ramp.

"I don't think I can hold it any longer," said Regan as he drove into the rest area parking as close as he could to the restroom facilities. "I'll be back in a minute."

Regan emerged from his car, stretching his muscles as he did. He had shut off the motor but had left the keys in the ignition, which was a fatal mistake. He completed his business in the restroom and came outside refreshed and ready to continue his trip. He yawned and stretched again, but he stopped in the middle of the exercise as he saw his car rolling up the on-ramp to the highway.

"What the hell!" exclaimed Regan as he realized that Mike Pearson was stealing his car. "Hey, come back here with my car, you bastard!"

Regan broke into a run as he tried so vainly to pursue

the stolen vehicle. He was out of breath when he reached the top of the ramp. He stood there panting as he watched the rear of his car disappear down the road.

"Shit!" he swore aloud.

The wind pushed against his back, and Regan remembered that his coat was still in the back seat of his car. He started walking, hoping to catch a ride from someone who would take him into the next town where he could call the state police. Better than that, he hoped for a state police car to come along.

Because it was a weekday, traffic on the interstate was light. Two cars and an eighteen-wheeler sped by his outstretched thumb as he continued walking. Deadman's Pass was fifteen minutes behind when a pickup truck finally stopped to give Regan a lift into Pendleton.

"Kind of a long way from no place, ain't yuh, son?" asked the old cowboy behind the wheel as Regan mounted the running board of what had to be the oldest pickup he had ever seen.

"I sure am, pardner," agreed Regan. "A hitchhiker stole my car back at that last rest area."

"Now if that don't beat all," twanged the cowboy. "Just goes to show yuh that yuh caint trust no one nowadays. Wull, git in, an' ah'll run yuh down to Pendleton to the state police post."

Regan managed to get the door open to the cab and to climb inside next to the cowboy. He felt the springs of the bench seat press against his buttocks as he squirmed to find a comfortable spot. Only the windshield had any glass in it, and the wind attacked him from all angles. He folded his arms in an attempt to retain some of his body heat.

"How long ago did this happen? Yer car bein' stole, ah mean."

"Over an hour ago."

"Whut wuz he? The hitchhiker who stole yer car, ah mean."

"He was just a kid from California."

"A long-haired hippie-type, ah'll bet. Yuh caint trust anyone with long hair, lessen o'course, it's a purty woman."

"You just might be right there, pardner."

"Whut kinda car did yuh have?"

"It's a Toyota, a blue Toyota."

"One o' them Jap jobbies, huh?"

"That's right."

The cowboy continued to jabber away at Regan the rest of the way to Pendleton, which was only fifteen miles away. Regan was grateful that it was not any farther than that.

The pickup screeched to a stop in front of the state police post. Regan thanked the old cowhand for the ride, and the old-timer said he hoped Regan got his car back and in one piece. They waved to each other, and the truck's wheels threw up gravel as it pulled away.

"I want to report my car being stolen," said Regan once he was inside the building.

"Stolen vehicle, huh?" said the patrolman as he looked up at Regan from his desk. "Why don't you have a seat over here by my desk, sir? You look like you could use a cup of coffee."

"I sure could," said Regan as he seated himself where the officer suggested.

"How do you want it?" asked the blue uniformed policeman.

"Just sugar. A teaspoon or two."

The patrolman brought the coffee and seated himself behind the desk. He opened the lower left drawer and

66

removed a printed form. Placing the form in front of him, he pulled a ball-point pen from his left shirt pocket.

Regan reached into his right hip pocket of his pants and removed his wallet. He took out his driver's license and his insurance card, which had the license plate number, serial number, and description of his car on it. He slid them across the desk toward the officer.

"I think you'll find most of the information you'll need on those," said Regan.

After copying the information he desired from the two cards, the patrolman began asking Regan the standard questions. When was the car stolen? What were the circumstances surrounding the theft? Can you give me a description of the suspect? Which direction did he drive off?

"Well, Mr. Regan," said the officer when he was finished with his interrogation, "he couldn't have gone too far, so I'll get these facts on the radio right away. We'll get your car back as soon as possible."

"I hope so," said Regan. "Well, since it's nearly dark, I think I'll get a room at that motel down the road. It doesn't look like I'm going to get to Portland tonight."

"No, sir, I guess not. If you'll wait a minute, I'll have a man drive you down to the motel."

Regan checked into the motel and informed the officer who had driven him there of the number of his room, just in case they wanted to call him if they found out anything about his car. That done, he went directly to his room where he undressed and fell into bed exhausted. He was soon asleep.

The sun had just crept over the horizon when a patrolman that Regan had not seen before knocked on his motel room door. Regan did not awaken until the second series of raps. He hustled into his pants and scrambled for the door.

"Mr. Thomas Regan?" queried the officer when Regan opened the door.

"Yes, I'm Tom Regan. Did you find my car?"

"Yes, sir, we did, but you'd better finish getting dressed and come with me."

"Don't tell me that kid wrecked my car. That's all I need now."

"Your vehicle did sustain some damage, Mr. Regan, but it's still operable."

"That's good news. Did you catch that crazy kid?"

"We didn't have to look for him. He was found dead inside your car."

"Dead? How?"

"Someone shot him in the head."

"Holy shit! How did that happen?"

"The captain's hoping you can tell us about that."

Regan realized that he was being suspected of the murder. He stepped back into the room to finish dressing. The officer's words disturbed him.

First my car is stolen, he thought to himself, and now a murder. What next?

The state police had found Regan's car in the ditch alongside U.S. highway 395 south of Pendleton. The officer who made the discovery had approached it with his gun out and ready, but he had had no need of it because Mike Pearson was long dead. The windows had been rolled up tight, but the one in the driver's door had been shattered by a single bullet; the same one that had entered Pearson's head just above his left ear. The officer had found Pearson sprawled over the passenger seat. The victim had probably died instantly, because the officer had found very little blood on the seat. The

68

car had evidently been moving when the shot had been fired because it was entrenched in deep mud in the ditch. No clues had been found that might lead to the murderer.

"It's our guess, Mr. Regan," said the state police captain, "that the killer pulled his car alongside yours and shot Pearson through the window. The coroner says he died around seven o'clock last night, which means the killer probably couldn't make out who he was shooting at. The dash lights probably gave him a silhouette for a target, and he shot Pearson from close range. He shot Pearson for one of two reasons. One, he was either a maniac with an uncontrollable desire to commit murder; or two, he was out to get you and mistook Pearson for you."

"Or three," said Regan, "the killer could have been after Pearson all along. He did steal my car, and he told me he was trying to get away from his girl in Idaho. She could've killed him."

"I don't think so, Mr. Regan. I think the killer wanted you. Do you know if anyone wants you dead?"

"A few jealous husbands maybe, but I don't think any of them would follow me all the way to Oregon."

"What about your line of work? I understand that you're a reporter."

"Newspaper writer," Regan said, correcting the captain. "Yeah, I supposee that could have something to do with it, but I kind of doubt it."

"Why?"

"Because only a handful of people know about the story I'm working on, and they're all on my side. At least, I think they are."

"What kind of story are you working on?"

"I'm following up a new lead on Lee Harvey Oswald.''

''Oswald? The guy that shot Kennedy?''

''Supposedly shot Kennedy. It has yet to be proven beyond a shadow of a doubt that he did it.''

''Oh, I suppose you're one of those who thinks that Kennedy was the victim of a conspiracy. I don't buy that theory myself.''

''Then why have all those witnesses died in such mysterious ways?''

''I'm not interested in that,'' rebuked the captain. ''I'm only concerned about Pearson's murder. Since the shooting occured while you were just down the road, you're in the clear.''

''I'm certainly glad to hear you say that.''

''That doesn't mean a thing. I still think someone wants you dead.''

''I've told you all I know,'' said Regan.

''Except who would want to kill you.''

''If I knew that, I'd tell you.''

''Okay, Mr. Regan, but if someone is trying to kill you, would you mind going to another state to have it done? We've already got enough murders.''

''I'll try to oblige you, Captain. Now what about my car?''

''We're finished with it. A tow truck is bringing it in now. I'll have a man run you down to the garage to pick it up. You'll have to pay the towing charge, of course.''

''Of course,'' said Regan as he stood up to leave.

After waiting around half the day for his car to be repaired, Regan was on his way to Vancouver, which was across the Columbia River from Portland. He checked into a motel in the Washington city as soon as he arrived there. He opened the telephone directory in his room to find that Vancouver had only four

Crowells listed. None of them, however, had the first name of Robert or the initials "RD". He did find one that had the same address as the one on the list he had gotten from Hewitt. He called the number in the book.

"Hello, my name is Tom Regan, and I'm trying to locate a Robert Delano Crowell who used to live here in Vancouver. Would you happen to know him?"

"Yes, I do," answered the voice of an elderly woman. "What do you want with Robbie?"

"I'm a newspaper writer, and I want to interview Mr. Crowell for a story I'm doing."

"I suppose it's another one of those stories about Vietnam," said the lady. "Why can't you people leave him alone? Isn't it bad enough that he lost an arm and the use of his legs serving his country? Why do you people have to keep reminding him that he's a cripple? Can't you leave him alone?"

Regan was caught off guard by her sudden attack. He was perplexed about how to fend off her onslaught.

"Uh, Mrs. Crowell? You are his mother, aren't you?"

"Yes, I am, and damn proud of it."

"I'm sure you are, Mrs. Crowell, but I didn't know about your son's injuries." He paused to let that sink in. "I only wanted to talk to him for a few minutes about some of his past experiences; ones before Vietnam."

"Oh, that's different," she said. "I'm sorry, Mister— What did you say your name was?"

"Regan, ma'am. Tom Regan."

"I'm sorry, Mr. Regan. I just assumed you knew about his arm and legs. I didn't mean to be so harsh. If you'll hold on, I'll ask Robbie if he wants to talk with you."

Regan waited.

"Hello?" said a man's voice. "This is Bob Crowell. Can I help you?"

"Mr. Crowell, my name is Tom Regan. I'm a writer for *The Morning Sun* in Phoenix, Arizona. I was wondering if I could come over and interview you for a story I'm doing."

"You're from Phoenix?"

"Yes, sir, I am."

"You've come a long way, and just to talk to me?"

"Yes, sir, I have."

"Well, I suppose it would be rude to send you away without giving you what you came for, so why don't you drop by?"

"What time would be convenient for you, sir?"

"Right now would be okay. You could stay for supper, that is, of course, if you like fried chicken."

"I love it," said Regan. "How do I get there?"

Crowell gave him the directions, and Regan was at the house twenty minutes later.

Robert Crowell was one of the thousands of victims of the Vietnam War. He had been a captain when his unit invaded the Demilitarized Zone in 1967. A North Vietnamese mortar shell had severed his left arm from the shoulder, and a fragment of the same shell had lodged in his spine, paralyzing him from the waist down. In spite of his physical injuries, his mental attitude was good. He displayed none of the bitterness that so often accompanies disabling injuries. Regan found him to be openly friendly and charmingly hospitable.

"I've often thought about taking up a career as a writer," said Crowell from his wheelchair across the table from Regan. "My only problem is I wouldn't know what to write about."

72

"That should be the least of your problems," said Regan. "Your past experiences should be a very fertile field for creativity."

"The trouble with that is no one wants to be reminded of Vietnam."

"Maybe not," said Regan, "but it wouldn't hurt to try. What have to got to lose?"

"Nothing, I suppose, but what would I do for an encore?"

"Use your imagination. You could take one little incident out of your career, exaggerate its importance in the scheme of things, and create a mystery. The possibilities are limitless."

"I see what you mean," said Crowell. "Thanks. I just might do that. Now what can I do for you?"

"I happen to be interested in one of those little incidents from your career in the Marines."

"Such as?"

"Such as a night in 1959 when you were stationed at Cubi Point."

"Oh?"

"Did you know Lee Harvey Oswald back then?"

Crowell burst out laughing. He rubbed his eyes with the index finger and thumb of his hand. He smiled as he shook his head at Regan.

"Excuse me, Mr. Regan, but I had to laugh. I had almost forgotten about Oswald. You're the first person who's ever asked me about him."

"Then you did know him?"

"No, not really. The only contact I ever had with him was on that night in 1959 that you mentioned. I was the Officer of the Day that night in February. Anyway, I think it was February. That watch was just changing about midnight. Oswald was on guard duty."

"Oswald was on guard duty?" interrupted Regan.

"No, let me correct that. He was just going on watch when he found that the man he was to relieve had been shot with his own gun. Oswald reported it, and I went out to investigate. The wounded man —"

"Wounded? He wasn't dead?"

"No, just wounded. His name was Schramm, I think. Anyway, I had him taken to the dispensary, and that was the last I saw of him. I questioned Oswald about the incident. All he could tell me was that he had found Schramm with a bullet in his head."

"Schramm was shot in the head?"

"Yeah, he had blood all over his face. Someone had apparently taken his piece away from him, then shot him with it. Figuring that he was dead or that he heard Oswald coming, the assailant left the scene."

"Someone must've heard the shot. Didn't Oswald say he had heard a shot?"

"No, I don't think so. Come to think of it, I don't think I ever asked him that question. Anyway, no one was ever caught for the shooting."

"What happened to Schramm?"

"I guess he recovered and was sent back over to Japan. At least that's what I heard later. I got this report saying that he had attempted suicide and that he was being sent to another base for court-martial."

"Suicide?"

"That's what it said."

"Did you ever see his face?"

"Just when it was covered with blood."

Regan reached inside his coat and removed the picture of Schramm from the pocket. He handed it across the table to Crowell.

"Did he look like this?"

"This is Oswald," said Crowell in a matter of fact way.

"No, Mr. Crowell, that is Phil Schramm, the man who was shot that night at Cubi Point."

Crowell was astounded by Regan's statement.

"Are you sure? This man looks just like Oswald did back then."

"That's who I thought it was, too, when I first saw this photograph." Crowell returned the picture to Regan. "My brother-in-law served with Schramm. He took this picture in 1958. He knew him personally. He's swears that this is Phil Schramm."

"That's incredible, but I don't get it. What has all this to do with what Oswald did later in his life? I mean killing President Kennedy."

"This man may have been a double for Oswald. You're not the only person who identified the man in this picture as Oswald. That makes me want to find Schramm if he is still alive."

"Why?"

"Another writer wrote a book about the assassination of John Kennedy. He alludes to certain facts that Oswald could have had a double who posed as Oswald in Dallas the last few weeks before the assassination. Schramm may have been that double."

"Now I see what you're after," said Crowell.

"Do you remember who was in charge of the investigation of the shooting?"

"The Navy handled it. A commander from Naval Intelligence came snooping around for a few days. His name was Bertram, Lt. Com. Bertram. I never got his first name. As I recall, he left about the same time that Schramm was shipped to Japan."

"Are you sure that was his name?"

"Positive," assured Crowell. "I'll never forget him because he was such a comical little guy. He had a strange way of talking; his voice had a high, nasal pitch to it. It was hard to keep a straight face when talking with him because that voice and that tubby gut of his were almost too much to handle."

So Bertram had a funny voice and a fat belly, Regan thought to himself.

"I want to thank you, Mr. Crowell," said Regan as he pushed himself away from the table. "You've been very helpful, and the meal was terrific."

"I'm glad you enjoyed it," said Crowell. He turned his wheelchair away from the table in order to escort Regan to the door.

"There is one more thing," said Regan. "I think it would be wise if you didn't tell anyone about me being here."

"Why?"

"Someone tried to kill me yesterday. I think they wanted to keep me from talking to you. From what you've told me, they may want you dead, too."

"Cut it out, will you? You're scaring the hell out of me."

"Sorry about that," said Regan at the door.

"Why do you think they may want me, too?"

"You know that Schramm didn't die that night at Cubi Point."

"H-mm, I see what you mean. You can count on me; I won't say a word to anyone."

"At least not till you hear from me," warned Regan one more time.

"Got it!"

They shook hands, and Regan returned to his motel room to call Milt Harris in Phoenix.

"Hello, Mr. Harris, this is Tom Regan."

"Regan? Where the hell are you?"

"Vancouver, Washington."

"Washington? I thought you were going to Salt Lake City?"

"I've already been there."

"Why didn't you call me from there?"

"There wasn't anything important to report from there."

"You mean you didn't find that writer?"

"Oh, yeah, I found Hewitt."

"And?"

"And he is working on a book about Oswald."

"Have you found out anything significant yet?"

"Could be-e-e."

Regan could picture in his mind Milt Harris doing a slow burn as he squirmed in his chair.

"Well, what the hell are you waiting for? Tell me what you've learned."

"Have you got your tape recorder on?"

"Yes, dammit."

"Okay, here goes. When I talked to Hewitt, he seemed to be on the level. He admitted calling my brother-in-law, but he denied every having called Mrs. Bagdonovich. I found out that he has a list of people who knew Oswald when Oswald was in the Marines. That list is divided between his three research assistants who in turn track down the present whereabouts of the people on their share of the list. He told me the name and address of the girl who has my brother-in-law on her list. She also happens to have Paul Bagdonovich on her list. Anyway, I paid her a little visit. I didn't get much out of her, but her roomie was quite co-operative. Anyway, Cindy, the roommate, told me that Hewitt has a lot of money, but she doesn't know where he gets it from. You'd never know he was well-heeled by the house he lives in.

"After that, I headed up here to find a guy named Crowell who was on the list that Hewitt gave me. I figured he must've been important because Hewitt had put some initials after his name. On the way here, a hitchhiker I'd picked up stole my car. The state police found my car and the kid who'd taken it. The only thing wrong with that was someone had put a bullet into the kid's brain. The police think the killer was after me."

"Hey, this is starting to get good," interrupted Harris.

"Don't get too excited yet; I'm still alive."

"A guy can hope, can't he?"

"Don't make any bets on it," said Regan.

"What about this Crowell?"

"I found Crowell here in Vancouver," continued Regan. "He had been the Officer of the Day the night that Schramm was shot. He identified the picture of Schramm as Oswald. What's more, he told me that Schramm wasn't killed at Cubi Point. He was only wounded and shipped off to Japan. He said he had seen a report from Naval Intelligence that said Schramm had attempted suicide. Then he told me who had been the investigating officer from Naval Intelligence. You'll never guess what his was."

Regan paused to add suspence to his narrative.

"Are you going to tell me or not?" growled Harris.

"What, no guesses?"

"Regan!"

"Okay, already. You don't have to yell. I'll tell you. His name was Bertram."

"Bertram? Isn't that the name of the other writer who

78

called Bagdonovich?''

"You got it, Red Rider. That isn't all. The description Crowell gave me of Bertram fits Hewitt."

"I'll be damned."

"Not yet, Mr. Harris. Tomorrow, I'm going to get a copy of Hewitt's book from the library. It's bound to have a picture of him on the back of the jacket. If it does, I'm going back over to see Crowell. If he identifies Hewitt as Bertram, then I'll be positive that I'm on to something or someone."

"Then what?''

"Then I'm on my way back to Salt Lake City to see a certain big-bellied man about his career in the Navy."

VII

Salt Lake City

February 21, 1977

Regan parked his car four doors down and across the street from Hewitt's house. He saw Hewitt's wife drive out of the driveway and then proceed in the other direction from which his car was pointed. He figured Hewitt must be alone in the house.

There's only one way to find out for sure, Regan thought.

The wind hipped his ears as he climbed out of his car. He pulled the collar of his coat up around his ears as he walked toward the front door to Hewitt's house. A light was shining from the window that Regan supposed was the one in Hewitt's study.

"You'd better be here," Regan muttered aloud as he knocked on the door.

Seconds later, the door opened, and Hewitt smiled out at Regan standing on the porch.

"Why, Mr. Regan, how nice to see you again."

"Yeah, I'll bet," Regan snarled. "Aren't you a little surprised to see me alive?"

"Why whatever do you mean?"

"Cut the crap, Hewitt. Or is it Bertram?"

Hewitt's eyes widened as he gasped.

"Yeah, I thought so, you little mole," said Regan as he forced his way inside by pushing Hewitt back away from the doorway. "You lying little creep! You tried to have me killed. I can't prove it, but I know it had to be you."

Regan slammed the door behind him.

"What are you talking about?" squeaked Hewitt.

"I said to cut the crap, Hewitt," said Regan as he slapped Hewitt across the face. "Now I want some straight answers, and I want them fast."

"I'll tell you anything you want to know," whined Hewitt, "but please don't hit me again. I bruise very easily."

"So do peaches," retorted Regan. "And to think that you were in Naval Intelligence."

"Then you know?"

"Not everything, pal, but I've got a feeling I'm about to find out a lot more than I knew the last time we had a little chat."

"Let's go into my study, and I'll tell you everything I can."

Hewitt retreated toward the workroom, and Regan followed close behind, making certain that Hewitt was not going after a gun or some other weapon. Hewitt waddled toward his chair, but Regan pushed him toward the sofa instead.

"Sit over there where I can watch you better."

Hewitt obeyed the command as Regan turned the desk chair around to face the sofa.

"Before I begin to tell my story," said Hewitt in a calmer tone, "would you tell me how you found out that I had once used the name of Bertram?"

"Robert Crowell identified your picture on the back of your book. He knew you as Lt. Cmdr. Bertram of Naval Intelligence when you investigated the shooting of Phil Schramm."

"I see. That was eighteen years ago. I haven't used

that name since.''

''Oh, no? How about when you called Paul Bag-donovich in December? You used it then.''

''No, Mr. Regan, I did not. Someone else did.''

''Oh, really? And who was that?''

''I don't know, but I'm as anxious as you are to find out. He may have been the person who has tried to kill me as well as you.''

''Oh, sure,'' said Regan. ''Will you cut it?''

''I swear to you that I don't know who that person could be.''

''Then tell me what you do know. You can start with Schramm, Oswald, and Bertram back in 1959.''

''I wasn't in the Navy at the time of the shooting. I had been in Naval Intelligence until I was discharged in May of 1958. After that, I was with the CIA. I was working on the U-2 flights from our base at Atsugi, Japan. Some enlisted men had accidentally walked into a hangar one day where we kept the U-2. We were afraid they might accidentally tell the wrong people about what they saw, so I assigned Schramm to keep an eye on them. They were, of course, your brother-in-law and Paul Bagdonovich.

''A third man made the same mistake a few weeks later. That was Oswald. I assigned another man to watch him. When he reported that Oswald was studying Russian, I came to the conclusion that Oswald was going to defect and tell the Russians about the U-2's. Later, I found out that I was wrong with my conclusion.

''In the meantime, Schramm reported that O'Toole and Bagdonovich did not talk about what they had seen that day in the hangar. After more thorough checking into their backgrounds, I decided that further surveillance of their activities was unnecessary. Neither man was the type who would betray his country. I decided to remove Schramm from their midst.

"However, I still had Oswald to contend with. We had to do something to stop him from selling out to the Russians. It was decided by higher authorities that he should be eliminated. Schramm was assigned the task, but our plan failed.

"Schramm was on guard duty at Cubi Point on a night in February 1959. Oswald had the watch after him. The plan was for Schramm to shoot Oswald when he came on duty. Naturally, he would be caught, but Schramm was supposed to say that he had mistaken Oswald for a Filipino insurrectionist who was trying to sneak into the camp. We would then try Schramm before a military court, find him guilty, and then ship him off to prison. In reality, we would have just changed his name, and he would have been assigned to another station. Schramm wasn't his real name, so it wouldn't have been hard to change it."

"Wait a minute!" exclaimed Regan. "What do you mean his name wasn't Schramm?"

"No, that was his CIA name. I don't know what his real name was. I may have seen it once or twice, but I can't recall what it was."

"That's very interesting, but go on about what happened at Cubi Point."

"Like I was saying, the plan to kill Oswald failed. Schramm had only wounded him on the left side of his head. He was about to finish the job when another Marine came along. For some strange reason, Schramm decided to change identities with Oswald because he knew that they looked so much alike. Whatever possessed him to do such a crazy thing no one will ever know. He switched dog tags and rifles with Oswald, and that began the masquerade.

"Oswald was taken to the hospital where he started to recover from his wound. To keep him from talking, we kept him drugged. It was while he was under the influence of sodium pentathol that I discovered that I had been mistaken about him. I learned that he was extremely patriotic with a desire to do more for his country. He was studying Russian as well as Spanish and French in order to become an interpreter and possibly enter the intelligence branch of the military.

"Now I couldn't very well let a young man like him be wasted, and the Company was in need of new recruits; therefore, I decided that he should become one of my operatives. He literally leaped at the opportunity when I presented it to him. The problem then was what to do with him since Schramm was masquerading as him. Oswald suggested that I transfer him, but I had to have a reason for that. He reminded me that he had accidentally shot himself with a .22 caliber derringer the previous year when he was in Japan. A court-martial could be convened, and he could be found guilty, which would necessitate a transfer. It was a sound idea; therefore, it was done. Schramm was tried as Oswald, found guilty, then transferred to El Toro, California. Only the real Oswald arrived at El Toro. Schramm was sent to Florida. It was decided by higher-ups that because of their uncanny resemblance to each other they should be separated by as much distance as possible.

"That was the last I saw of either of them until I saw Oswald on television after John Kennedy's death. I was shocked that Oswald had had anything to do with it. He had been so patriotic. It truly disturbed me to think of him as an assassin.

"When I read some books about the assassination

and their authors suggested that Oswald was innocent, I decided to go into it further than they had. I have become convinced that Oswald was a scapegoat for more sinister elements, and that made me determined to write about his life. In the book, I hope to prove that he was innocent of the crime that history has blamed him for.

"As to the recent events surrounding you, Mr. Regan, I am in near total ignorance about them. I know nothing of your activities with the exception of what you yourself have told me. I have no ideas about who would want you dead. Certainly not I. The information that you have gleaned thus far is extremely valuable to me. Especially valuable is your brother-in-law's picture of Schramm. That is the leading evidence that Oswald had a double."

"Wrong, Hewitt," corrected Regan. "You are; you're the only person who knows that Oswald had a double. At least, you're the only one I've found so far."

"Yes, I see what you mean."

"Do you?" Regan glared at the round little man with the pale skin. "I'm almost inclined to believe you, but why didn't you tell me the truth before?"

"Would you have believed me?"

"I might have," said Regan. He tossed Hewitt's tale around in his head. "Okay, I believe you now. I guess that means we're working on the same side, which means whoever tried to kill me is going to try to kill you, too."

"I've already told you that an attempt was made on my life. Someone drained the fluid from the brakes on my car. Fortunately, the accident that resulted from the incident was a minor one. No one was hurt."

"Lucky for you."

"Yes, it was. My wife was driving the car at the time."

"Okay, enough about that," said Regan. "Let's start planning on where we go from here. In order to prove Oswald innocent, his steps will have to be traced all the way up to his capture in Dallas. You said you were in the CIA and that Oswald worked for you. That fact will have to be corroborated by another CIA boss. Who did he work for in California?"

"I only knew the man by his code name, which was Pressler. We had met a few times while we were both still in the Company, but I have seen him once since then. That was in 1962 after so many of us were shuffled about or dismissed from the Company. Pressler had taken a position as a security agent for some of the downtown hotels in Las Vegas."

"You didn't get his real name then?"

"No, it was an unspoken rule of Company employees not to question each other about our true identities."

"That's going to make finding him a little tough. Can you tell me anything about him?"

"The man made me uncomfortable when we talked, and he appeared to be uncomfortable being with me. It was only a quick reunion. I saw him sitting alone in the restaurant of the Four Queens Hotel. He was in a corner booth having coffee. We talked for a few minutes before he excused himself."

"Have you tried to find him since you started this book?"

"No, I've been concentrating on finding everyone who might have known both Oswald and Schramm while they were in the Orient."

"Okay, I'll find Pressler for us. What did he look like the last time you saw him?"

"Pressler is about five feet six inches tall, black hair, ruddy complexion, and brown eyes that can stare right through you. He appeared to be a very clean and neat individual."

"That's not much to go on, but if he's still in Vegas, I'll find him."

Both men fell silent with thought.

"Is there anything else you want to tell me about Pressler or the incident in the Philippines?"

"I believe I've covered it all."

"Okay, Hewitt, I'm going to buy your story for now, but God help you if you're lying."

"I swear to you," sighed Hewitt, "that I have told you the truth as I know it."

Regan stood up to leave. Hewitt struggled to his feet. They stood looking at each other, as if they wanted to be reassured of each other's integrity.

"Okay," said Regan as he extended his hand to Hewitt. "No hard feelings about the slap in the face?"

The rotund little man smiled back at the taller writer. He reached for Regan's hand, and his lips started to form the syllables of forgiveness just as a bullet crashed through the study window and into the side of Hewitt's head above his right ear. Splinters of glass from the shattered pane tore at Regan's hand and face, and blood from Hewitt's wound spattered on his coat.

Regan was frozen for an instant as the realization of what was happening struck him. Hewitt's hand had clutched his with a death grip. The convulsing movement of the dead man's body pulled Regan off balance jerking him to the dead man's left as a second bullet sprayed more glass around the room. He felt a sharp pain at the back of his head as his eyes rolled back, and he fell unconscious over Hewitt's body.

Mrs. Hewitt found them minutes later when she returned from shopping. Regan was still bleeding slightly. Although unconscious, he was at least alive. Her husband was dead. He had inadvertently saved Regan's life by pulling him down.

Despite her initial revulsion Mrs. Hewitt was able to control herself long enough to call the police and report the murder. The police arrived in minutes. The uniformed officers ordered two ambulances sent to the house. One removed Hewitt's body to the morgue as the other rushed Regan to a nearby hospital for treatment.

The wound to his head was superficial, having only creased his skull. It had spilled a large amount of his blood, but the bullet had failed to penetrate the occipital bone in the back of his head. He had been very lucky. Another two inches to the front and the bullet would have killed him as surely as the one that had halted Hewitt's life.

After stitching up the wound and placing a pressure bandage around his head, the doctor had revived Regan long enough to make certain that he was going to recover. They placed him in a prone position on an intensive care bed where they moved him from the emergency room. He had lost consciousness again.

It was nearing midnight when the pain from his head awakened him. He groaned as he reached for his wound, but then remembered how he had received the injury. He opened his eyes and quickly realized that he was in a hospital room. The ward was dimly-lit.

"Nurse?" he called out. His mouth was dry, and his throat was sore.

"Yes, Mr. Regan?" asked the nurse who was sitting on a stool next to his bed.

Regan turned his head in the direction of her voice. He could see her white-stockinged legs. So far, so good, he thought. He continued turning his head until he could see the hem of her uniform. It was high above her knees. Getting better, he thought. His view travelled the rest of the way up her white dress to see a farily pretty woman of about thirty-five.

"Not too shabby," he muttered aloud.

"What did you say?" she asked as she leaned closer to him. Her movement permitted Regan to gaze inside the open top of her uniform. He was gratified to find that her breasts appeared to still be firm although supported by a bra.

"Have I died and gone to heaven?"

"No, you're still among the living," she replied.

"Good," he said. "There's still hope for us."

"For some of us," she corrected. "How's your head feeling?"

"Like someone hit me with a hammer."

"I'll give you something for the pain."

"Not yet. I have to think first. Where's Hewitt?"

"If you mean the other man who was shot," said the nurse, "he was taken to the morgue."

"Oh, shit!" cursed Regan. "He's dead!"

"Please, Mr. Regan, you mustn't excite yourself."

"Too late. You've already done that for me." He rolled over on his side. "Where's the nearest telephone?"

"You're in no condition to use a telephone right now," she said as she moved closer to him.

"I don't want to hear that," he argued. "I want to hear the dial-tone from a receiver. Now where is it?"

Regan moved as if he was going to get out of bed, but the nurse blocked his path. He started to argue further with her, but he saw two men enter the room at that moment. The older one was wearing a white coat, which told Regan that he had to be a doctor. The other younger man followed him toward the bed. He was wearing an overcoat, as if he was trying to look like Dick Tracy. His little mustache made him look more like Fearless Fosdick.

"Something wrong, Miss Kramer?" asked the doctor.

"Dr. Taylor," said the surprised nurse. "Mr. Regan is awake and complaining of severe pain."

"Then give him something for it," said the doctor.

"Yes, sir," said Miss Kramer as she moved toward her station narcotics cabinet.

"I don't need anything right now," said Regan.

Dr. Taylor and the detective moved closer to the bed. The doctor displayed his best bedside manner smile, but the policeman was very grim.

"Mr. Regan, I'm Lt. Crain of the Murray Police Department." He flashed a badge for Regan. "I'd like to ask you a few questions if you feel up to it."

"I think I can handle it," said Regan.

"Good," said Crain as he warmed to the occasion. "Can you tell me what happened?"

"Let's see," said Regan. "You're going to ask me what I was doing at Hewitt's in the first place, so I'd better start from there."

"You've seen too many cop shows on television," said Crain. Dr. Taylor laughed.

"Too many medical shows, too," said Regan as he glared at the doctor. Taylor glared back.

"Then start by telling me what you were doing at Hewitt's house."

"In case you haven't checked my wallet," said Regan.

"We have," said Crain, "and we know you're a reporter."

"A newspaper writer," corrected Regan.

"Whatever," said Crain.

"Well, Hewitt was working on a book about Lee Harvey Oswald, and I was there to interview him."

"Mrs. Hewitt said you had been there before."

"That's right. Last week. I went back to get some further information about his work."

Crain seemed satisfied with that answer.

"Anyway, we were talking about his book when someone shot us through the window. That's all there is to it."

"Why did you park you're car so far away from the house?"

This guy is smarter than I thought, Regan conceded to himself.

"I'd only been to the house once before," said Regan. "I drove by it in the dark. When I realized my mistake, I just parked where it was at instead of turning around and going back."

He bought it, thought Regan.

"You can't remember anything else?"

"That's it, lieutenant."

"It isn't much, but it'll have to do for now."

"Lieutenant, it's your turn to tell me what happened to Hewitt and me."

"Okay, Mr. Regan," said Crain. "I suppose you have a right to know. From what we've been able to find at the scene of the shootings, an unknown assailant fired two shots through the window, killing Hewitt and wounding you. We don't know what caliber of weapon was used, but it was fired from just outside the window because we found traces of gun powder on the glass fragments. The killer couldn't have been more than six feet from the window. He must've used a silencer because none of the neighbors we've talked to reported hearing any gunshots. There were no distinguishable footprints near the window or on that side of the house. We didn't find any shell casings, which leads me to believe the killer used a revolver; a .38 or .45 caliber. That's all we have so far."

"I hope you find the bastard who shot me," said Regan.

"We will, Mr. Regan. Have you got any ideas about who would want to kill either of you?"

"Sorry, but I don't."

"Well, if you remember anything that might be important, have the nurse call me immediately."

"Speaking of calling people," said Regan as he propped himself up on his right elbow, "can you do something about getting me a phone?"

"Dr. Taylor will have to okay that," said Crain.

"I don't see that it would cause any harm," said Taylor. "Miss Kramer, get Mr. Regan a phone."

Kramer was gone only a minute before returning with a white extension phone. She handed the receiver to Regan, then plugged the cord into the wall-jack near the head of his bed.

"Is it a local call?" she asked Regan.

"No, I want to call my boss in Phoenix." He could read her next question in her eyes. "Collect."

The nurse dialed nine to get an outside line, then zero to get the operator. When Regan heard the operator's voice, he placed the collect call to Milt Harris who reluctantly accepted the charges to his home telephone.

"Regan, what are you doing calling me collect at my

home?''

"Stuff it, Harris. I'm in no mood to quibble over money, especially your money. I want a raise, and I want it retroactive to the day I started with *The Morning Sun*."

"A raise? Are you crazy?"

"Funny you should ask. Yeah, a raise. You can call it hazardous duty pay."

"What are you talking about?"

"Someone tried to kill me again."

Regan's last statement raised Crain's eyebrows considerably. He made a mental note to check into Regan's background and his recent activities.

"Where are you now?" ask Harris.

"I'm in a hospital bed in Salt Lake. The killer nearly turned out my lights permanently this time."

"How?"

"I'll give you the details when I'm feeling better. Now what about that raise?"

"You got it."

"Good for me. I'll call again when we can talk more privately."

"Oh, no, you don't. Tell me what happened."

"Someone shot me while I was talking to Hewitt at his house tonight. The killer only wounded me. Hewitt wasn't that lucky. He's dead."

"Were you able to get any information from Hewitt before he died?"

"Yeah, but we can discuss it later. A pretty nurse is waiting to stick my ass with a needle." He smiled up at Miss Kramer. "I think I'm in love."

"You don't have time to fool around with any nurses," said Harris. "You've got a story to work on."

"All work and no play makes Tom Regan a horny old

goat like you."

"If you weren't on to something big, I'd fire you for that remark."

"No, you wouldn't," said Regan. "I'll talk to you tomorrow or the next day."

Regan handed the receiver to Miss Kramer who removed the telephone from the room. She returned to administer the narcotic injection she had prepared. Dr. Taylor and Lt. Crain wandered off to the nurses station for a private conversation. They were gone when Regan looked up after getting his shot.

"Why don't you lean back and relax?" said Miss Kramer. "The shot should take effect in a few minutes."

"Have you got a first name?" asked Regan.

"Nancy," she said.

"Okay, Nancy," said Regan as he relaxed. "You'd better take good care of me because I'm about to solve the crime of the century."

An exaggeration, thought Regan, but it got me to first base.

He was soon asleep.

VIII

Las Vegas

March 1, 1977

Downtown Las Vegas was back to its usual self when Regan and Bill Davis arrived there the last night of February. Many of the light displays of the hotels had been turned off during the recent energy crisis, but they were going full-tilt when Regan pulled his car into the parking building behind the Four Queens Hotel. Each man carried his own bag as they walked to the rear entrance of the hotel.

Regan had spent four additional days in the hospital following the shooting at Hewitt's. There had been neither a skull fracture nor a concussion as a result of the shot that creased his skull. The doctor had wanted to keep him an extra day, but Regan had insisted on being released. He had promised Dr. Taylor that he would not return to his travels for at least three more days.

Cindy Perkins and Valerie Davis had heard over the radio about the shooting at Hewitt's. They had both been relieved to hear that Regan had not died with Hewitt. They had given Mrs. Hewitt their condolences and had attended Cal Hewitt's funeral. They had also made it a point to visit Regan every day and night that he was in the hospital.

"You're going to spend some time with me," said Cindy the last night she visited Regan. "I insist that you

95

stay with me this weekend. You'll need someone to look after you while you're recuperating."

"I don't know," said Regan. "Salt Lake City doesn't seem too healthy this week."

"Things will change for the better," said Cindy into his ear. "I promise."

The Murray police had impounded Regan's car for the duration of his stay in the hospital. Dr. Taylor arranged with Lt. Crain for it to be held until the following Monday. Regan was not too pleased by their action, but he was powerless to do anything about it. He had planned to leave for Las Vegas as soon as he was released from the hospital that Saturday morning. Since the police were holding his car, he was forced into staying with Cindy and Valerie.

When he and Cindy arrived at the apartment, they found Bill Davis talking to Valerie on the balcony outside the apartment door. Their conversation appeared to be friendly from a distance. Valerie was smiling, and Bill Davis was leaning against the railing in a relaxed manner. They stopped talking when they saw Cindy and Regan approaching.

"What are you doing here, creep?" asked Cindy.

"Val told me that you were having a guest for the weekend," said Davis. His voice was deep and strong with a slight Texas accent. "I just came by to offer the gentleman my apologies for that regrettable little incident last week." Davis directed himself toward Regan. "I hope you can forgive me, Mr. Regan. I am deeply sorry."

Davis shoved out a large right hand toward Regan. Regan's first reaction was to take a step back because the sudden movement of a man with such an ominous look about him would frighten anyone.

"I can't blame you for that," said Davis as he let his hand sink slowly to his side.

"It's my turn to apologize," said Regan as he stepped forward and offered his hand in friendship.

"You don't know how good this makes me feel," said Davis as he gripped Regan's hand and pumped it vigorously. "It's mighty big of you to forgive me like this."

He's too friendly, thought Regan, but so are all big dogs.

"Yeah, well," stammered Regan, "I guess no real harm was done."

"And there isn't going to be neither," grinned Davis. "Val and I were just talking about you getting shot over at Hewitt's, and I got to thinking that you needed a bodyguard."

"Did you really think that up all by yourself?" sneered Cindy.

"I'm going to ignore that remark," said Davis, "because you don't know any better. That's why you're doing a man's job tending bar."

"And I'll ignore that remark," said Cindy, "because I already know what a chauvinistic pig you are."

"All right, you two," Valerie interceded.

"Right, Val," said Davis before returning to Regan. "Like I was saying before I was so rudely interrupted, I think you should have a bodyguard to keep you out of scrapes like you been going through this past week."

"Did you have anyone in mind?" asked Regan as if he did not already know the answer.

"Yeah, me," said Davis. "I'm good with my fists. . . ."

"Yes, I know," said Regan.

"And I handle a gun with respect."

"Terrific. While you're busy respecting your gun, some nut is filling me full of holes."

"I have a license to carry a gun, and I know my way around people who think they're tough."

"It might not be a bad idea," said Valerie. "Bill is also a karate expert."

"I'm beginning to get impressed," said Regan. "The more I hear, the more defenseless I feel."

"Then how about it?" asked Davis. "I'm sort of in between jobs right now, and the excitement would do me a lot of good."

"I'll give it some thought. How can I get in touch with you?"

"You won't have to worry about that because as long as you're staying here I'm going to be right here with you."

"There goes the weekend," said Cindy. "Who asked you anyway?"

"I did," said Valerie. "I didn't think it would hurt. After all, Bill does know how to protect himself. Why shouldn't he protect Tom, too?"

"I suppose," said Cindy.

That had just about settled the question. Davis spent most of the weekend at the apartment convincing Regan, and the writer began to appreciate Bill's few qualities. It was only a matter of time before Davis wore down Regan's initial dislike of having Davis for a bodyguard, but by Monday morning they had come to an agreement.

After a final check-up with Dr. Taylor, Cindy drove Regan and Davis down to the Murray police station. Lt. Crain called Dr. Taylor to confirm the fact that it was okay for Regan to drive again before he released Regan's car. Regan said good-bye to Cindy, promising to take care of himself and that he would come back to see her again. Minutes later, Regan had his car heading south on Interstate 15 for Las Vegas.

"This is where the action is," said Davis as they entered the casino of the Four Queens Hotel. "I can't wait to get to those tables."

"Don't let me hold you down," said Regan. "I'll check us in and bring you a key to the room."

"That sounds like a winner," said Davis as he gave his valise to Regan. "I'll be at the crap table."

Regan went upstairs to the lobby. He checked into the hotel under his own name although Davis had advised him to use a pseudonym. He took one key to their room on the eighth floor back down to Davis in the casino.

"It's going to be a hot time tonight," said Davis when Regan approached him. "Those bones are already rattling for me. Stick your money with mine, boy, and I'll make us both rich."

"No, I don't think so," said Regan. "I don't feel up to it tonight. Tomorrow maybe."

"Suit yourself. Don't wait up for me because I already saw a little something over there at a blackjack table that I'd like to get friendly with."

"Good luck," said Regan and then adding, "at both games."

Davis said something about luck not being involved, but Regan failed to catch all of what he said.

Regan stopped in the lobby to pick up their suitcases on his way to the room. Once in the room, he placed a long distance telephone call to Milt Harris in Phoenix.

"How are you feeling?" asked Harris.

"I'm beat into the ground. It was a long drive down here."

"That's why I think I'll fly up in the morning."

"What are you coming here for?"

"I know some people up there who might be able to help you."

"That's as good a reason as any," shrugged Regan. "Bring my paycheck with you. I'd like to spend a little of my own money for a change."

"That's another good reason for me to come up there. I don't think I should trust you with my credit cards in Sin City."

"So you don't trust me, huh? Then what am I doing with your credit cards in the first place?"

"If I had known you were going to be going to Vegas, I wouldn't have given them to you."

"Then you'd better hustle your ass up here because now I plan on spending a lot of money, mostly yours."

"Like hell, you are. I'll call you at the Queens as soon as I get in tomorrow."

Harris arrived at McCarran Field shortly after ten-thirty that morning, and Regan was on time to meet him at the terminal.

"It's nice to see you again," said Regan as he shook hands with Harris.

"I see you're still in one piece," replied Harris.

"I'm glad you noticed. Have you got my paycheck?"

"Is that all you can think about?"

"No, sometimes I think about sex and Einstein's Theory of Relativity. Since you're too old for one and you could care less about the other, I'm forced to speak in terms you understand. So where's my money?"

"If we weren't in a public place," said Harris as he reached into his inside coat pocket to retrieve the pay envelope, "I'd remind you who the boss really is." He shoved the envelope toward Regan. "Here! Don't spend it all in one place."

Regan snatched the envelope away from Harris, immediately ripping it open. He checked the amount payable first, then the deductions.

"Damned government sure takes a lot," he complained. "I suppose it'll have to do."

"There's more in this one," said Harris as he displayed a second envelope. "I managed to squeeze some expense money out of the company."

"Well, all right," said Regan as he reached for the cash.

"Not so fast, kid. Half of this is mine."

"So give me my half."

"Not till we get to the hotel. I'm staying at the Queens, too."

"Then let us be off. The tables are waiting."

"And they'll continue to wait. We're here on business. So let's get to it."

"We'll talk about it in the car."

Twenty minutes later they were stuck in traffic on their way downtown.

"Okay, tell me about this guy Pressler," said Harris.

"There isn't much more to tell than what I told you over the phone from Salt Lake the other day. Hewitt said his name Pressler was just a code name. He never knew him by his real name. It probably wouldn't do us any good anyway to know his real name, but we do have a fairly good physical description of our man."

"Did Hewitt tell you anything else about him?"

"He said that Pressler was working for a hotel security outfit."

"That narrows things down a bit. I happen to know a few people in security at the Four Queens. They may be able to help find our man."

"I guess you do have your uses, don't you?"

Harris slowly twisted his head to sneer at Regan who was smiling precociously.

"Where in the hell did you get that acid mouth?"

"From my mother. She's probably the greatest put-down artist I know. I almost believe she could cut down Christ if she felt he was getting too big for his breeches."

"If you say so," said Harris, "but in the meantime, try to remember that I'm the man who signs your paycheck."

"Whatever you say, 'Massa' Milt."

At the hotel, Regan accompanied Harris to his room. Harris tipped the bell-captain, then called his long-time friend Bradley McCauley who was the head of the Four Queens security department.

"Hello, Brad, this is Milt Harris."

"Milt, what are you doing up here in the middle of the week?"

"It's a business trip. I'm helping one of my 'cub' reporters," Harris glanced up at Regan, "on a story he's supposed to be handling on his own."

"I'll bet you're just using that as an excuse to get away from Phoenix for a few days."

"Not really, Brad. This could be a big story."

"Oh, really?"

"Yeah, and I was wondering if you have the time to come up to my room for lunch. We'd like to talk to you about this story."

"Sounds fascinating," said McCauley. "Where you at?"

Harris gave him the room number, and McCauley was knocking at the door ten minutes later.

Regan was slightly shocked when Harris introduced

him to McCauley. Although slightly older, McCauley looked the way Regan pictured Pressler. McCauley was shorter than Regan's five feet eleven inches, but he would be much shorter if he took off his high-heeled Italian boots, which would put McCauley down around the five feet six inches that Hewitt said Pressler stood. A commercial hair color restorer permitted only a little gray to show in McCauley's black hair. The sun had weathered his face into a leathery texture, which fit Hewitt's description of Pressler having a ruddy complexion. The real convincer was McCauley's eyes. They were almost black. Although they were quite friendly at the time of the introduction, Regan could tell that those eyes were capable of staring down men of great determination.

"Well, Milt," said McCauley, "what can I do to give you a hand with this story of yours?"

"I'll let Tom tell you," said Harris.

"Mr. McCauley, we're looking for a man who was formerly a CIA station head," said Regan as he watched McCauley closely for any signs that might confirm his suspicions. "He now works in the security department of a hotel here in Vegas. We don't know too much about him except his description and his code name when he was with the CIA."

Regan studied McCauley for any reaction. The only indication he gave that he was sensitive to the subject was a slight narrowing of his brow. Regan could feel McCauley's eyes begin to bore into him. He was discomforted, but he continued to pursue his prey.

"As far as we know, this man whose code name was Pressler has done no crime. Even if he had, that's not why we're interested in him."

McCauley's eyes came a little closer together with

the mentioning of the name Pressler, but they relaxed again when Regan said they were not looking to pin a crime on Pressler.

"The reason we want to talk to him is he might possess some information concerning Lee Harvey Oswald."

The eyes were confused as if they had mixed emotions over the mentioning of Oswald.

"We know that Oswald was assigned to Pressler in 1959 when Oswald was transferred to El Toro Marine Corps Air Station. What we want to know is whether or not Oswald went to Russia on his own. Only Pressler can tell us that."

McCauley was pensive. His eyes were penetrating deep into Regan's soul, and Regan was trying to gain this man's confidence by being as open as possible.

"You said you had a description," said McCauley.

"Yes, sir, Bertram said he was about your height," said Regan as he watched for McCauley's reaction to the name Bertram. "Pressler has brown eyes, black hair, and a ruddy complexion."

"That description is pretty old," said McCauley.

"How do you know that?" accused Regan.

McCauley was caught and he knew it.

"Because the last time I saw Bertram was 1962."

Milt Harris was stunned. His head jerked back noticeably, and his eyes volleyed back and forth from Regan to McCauley.

"How did you know I was Pressler?"

"I didn't," admitted Regan. "Nor did Milt. I had the description, and when you walked in, I got a hunch and played it."

"Remind me never to play cards with you," laughed McCauley. "Okay, what do you want to know about

Oswald?''

"Just tell me everything you can remember about him.''

"He wasn't with me very long,'' began McCauley, "but I got to know him quite well. He was a good kid in those days; one who wanted to do his patriotic duty for his country. I gave him minor assignments for the few months he was with me. He accepted them eagerly and without any questions. He wanted to go places with the Company, so he was eager to please.

"In the summer of '59, the Company requested a list of all agents who could speak Russian. Oswald was the only man I had who could, so I sent in his name. They checked him out and discovered that he knew about the U-2 flights over Russia. That and his court-martials made him the perfect defector as an embittered ex-Marine. The Company needed a new man inside Russia, and Oswald filled the bill.

"We arranged his discharge in September that year, and a few weeks later he was on his way to Russia. That was the last time I saw him in person, but I did speak with him on the phone when he returned to the States.

"I was already working here in Vegas and out of the Company, but he managed to find out where I was. He said his new boss had told him how to find me. I guess they were keeping an eye on all former agents at the time.

"Lee said he was a little upset with his new duty in New Orleans. It wasn't the town that bothered him, he said. It was the people he was working for. They weren't spies, he said. They were more like gangsters, and that worried him. I advised him to get out, but he said he didn't know what else he could do. After all, he did have that dishonorable discharge, which the Company had more or less forced on him.

"I could see his point, so I advised him to go to the FBI if he wanted to stay in the business. They were always looking for people to spy on the CIA for them. I told him he could gradually move from the Company to the Bureau, and that way no one would know that he was changing firms.

"He must've taken my advice because I got a call from Jack Cortland who was the Special Agent in Charge of the New Orleans office. Jack said that Lee had contacted him on my recommendation, and Jack wanted to know if I knew Lee. I told Jack that Lee had been working for me and that it was the Company that had sent him to Russia. I told him Lee would be a good man for the Bureau if they wanted to keep an eye on the Company in that area. Jack said he wanted to know if Oswald could be trusted. He wanted to be sure that Lee wasn't going to double-cross him like he was doing to the Company. I told him not to worry. Lee was all right.

"That was the last I heard of Lee until John Kennedy was shot in Dallas."

"Jack Cortland. Am I saying it right?" asked Regan.

"Yeah, that's right," said McCauley.

"Was that his real name?"

"Yeah, the Bureau didn't use code names the way the Company did. They didn't have as much to hide as we did in those days."

"Do you know where I can find Cortland?"

"Sure, I can. He lives in Garden Grove, California with his wife and kids. We're still friends. He quit the Bureau over the way they handled the investigation of Kennedy's murder. Would you like his address and phone number?"

"I'd appreciate it, Mr. McCauley," said Regan.

"You got it," said McCauley as he took a pen and notebook from the inside pocket of his suit coat. He wrote Cortland's name, address, and telephone number on a page. He tore out the page and handed it to Regan.

"You got a sharp boy here, Milt. I hope you're paying him what he's worth."

"Don't feed his ego, Brad. He doesn't need it. He's already into me for an arm and a leg."

Regan was not paying any attention to Milt's prattling. He still had more questions for McCauley.

"Mr. McCauley," said Regan as he put the notebook page in his inside coat pocket, "did you ever know an operative named Phil Schramm?"

"The name doesn't ring any bells," said McCauley. "Do you know anything else about him?"

"He was transferred to Florida about the same time that Oswald was sent to California."

"Hm-m. Did he have anything to do with the Cuban guerrilla camps down there? Because if he did, I may be able to help you again. There's a guy here in Vegas by the name of Joe Paris. He was mixed up with all that guerrilla stuff. He might've known the man you mentioned."

"Can you get in touch with him right away?"

"Sure," said McCauley. "I'll call him as soon as I get back to my office. I'll arrange a meeting so you can talk to him."

"That'd be great," said Regan.

"Is there anything else you want to know?"

"No, I guess that covers it."

"Then let's order lunch," said Harris. "I'm starved."

After they ate, McCauley returned to his office, and Regan and Harris drifted around the casino looking for a table without too many players. Regan had never played blackjack in Vegas, but Harris was a regular visitor to the gambling city. Living only 290 miles away in Phoenix, Harris could drive up there almost any weekend.

The dealers at the tables were relieved for their hourly breaks, and that started the movement of the players. Harris saw a dealer that he knew, and there happened to be some empty chairs at his table. The editor nudged Regan in that direction.

"Hello, Jesse," said Harris to the dealer.

"Hiya, Mr. Harris!" said Jesse, a dealer who never forgot the names of his heavy tippers. "How's it goin'?"

"I'm fine, Jess," said Harris. "How are you doing today?"

"I've been friendly all day," said Jesse.

"Sounds good enough to me," said Harris as he pulled out his wallet before seating himself at Jesse's table. "Sit down, Tom, and get out your money. Jesse here is going to show us a good time."

Regan did what Harris told him to do. Harris took a fifty from his wallet and slid it across the green felt to Jesse.

"Change fifty!" said Jesse.

"Who's he talking to?" asked Regan as he started to remove a twenty from his wallet.

"The pit boss," replied Harris as he stopped Regan's hand before he could get the twenty all the way out. "Don't be cheap, Tom. Take out a fifty."

"Hey, I'm not loaded like you," said Regan. "I have to work for my money."

"You little smart ass!" snapped Harris. "You do as I say, and Jesse will double that for you."

"If you say so," said Regan.

"I say so," said Harris with a smile as he watched Regan slide a fifty over to Jesse.

"Change fifty!" said Jesse to the pit boss, and the game began.

The two men stayed at the table until it was time for Jesse's break forty minutes later. They left when he left. Regan did not understand why they were leaving, but he did not complain either.

"How did you do?" asked Regan as they walked away from the row of tables.

"I'm up a couple of bets," said Harris.

"I won forty dollars," said Regan with pride.

"I suppose you think you're a big-time gambler now," sneered Harris. "You're a long way from it, kid. There's too many easy ways to lose your money."

"Oh, yeah?"

"Yeah, how do you think they built this place?"

Regan understood that.

"What do we do now?" asked Regan.

"Let's go get a cup of coffee."

They started for the restaurant downstairs, but they were stopped by the sound of Bill Davis calling out Regan's name.

Uh-oh, thought Regan. He was hoping that it was somebody other than Davis because he wanted to keep his bodyguard a secret from Harris.

"Hey, Tom," said Davis as he approached, "how come you ran off without telling me where you were going? You know you're not supposed to do that."

"I didn't want to disturb you," said Regan.

Harris stood by wondering who Davis was and waiting to be introduced to him. Regan was trying to avoid any introductions.

109

"Disturb me?" said Davis. "What the hell's a body-guard good for if he doesn't have a body to guard?"

"Bodyguard?" quizzed Harris. "What's this about a bodyguard, Regan?"

"I was going to tell you about that later, Mr. Harris. You see. . ."

"So you're Milt Harris?" interrupted Davis. "It's a pleasure to meet you, sir. The name is Bill Davis."

Davis threw out a paw, and Harris shook it reluctantly.

"Like I was saying," said Regan, "Bill and I met in Salt Lake City, and. . ."

"Yeah," said Davis as he interrupted again, "you might say we hit it off from the very start."

Davis let out a laugh that sounded more like the braying of an ass than anything else that Regan could think of. Regan covered his eyes as he shook his head slowly from side to side. Harris looked at Regan from the corner of one eye as the joke completely escaped him. Davis continued to bray until he realized that he was the only one laughing.

"I guess you don't get it," said Davis to Harris. "You see, the first time Tom and I saw each other we had this fight, and that's why I said we hit it off right from the start."

"What fight?" demanded Harris.

"I guess I forgot to tell you about it," said Regan. "If you'll let me explain, I'll tell you all about it."

"That might be a good idea," said Harris.

Davis suddenly became aware of the fact that he had talked out of turn. He looked apologetically in Regan's direction, but Regan was looking at the floor.

"You can tell me about it in the restaurant," said Harris as he turned down the stairs.

Over coffee, Regan told Harris without interruption from Davis about meeting Bill outside Cindy's and Valerie's apartment in Salt Lake City and about how Davis had volunteered to act as Regan's bodyguard until he was finished with his story.

"And you were going to do this for free?" asked Harris, although he was afraid of what the bottom line might be.

"Well, not exactly," said Davis. He looked at Regan for help.

"I was going to talk you into paying his expenses," said Regan to Harris. "I figured you'd want a live writer after I'm through with this story."

"You got it half right," said Harris. "I'd only want you alive long enough for me to kill you myself."

"Then that means you're willing to pay Bill's expenses?"

"You've got real balls, Regan," said Harris, laughing. "I've already had to re-finance my house to pay for your cockeyed story. . . ."

"The story of the century!" said Regan.

"And now you want me to get a part-time job to pay for his expenses. Tell me, Regan; why didn't you go to some other newspaper first?"

"You were the only game in town," said Regan.

"What else is new?" said Harris. "Okay, I'll pay, but you'd better keep him alive, Mr. Davis."

"Bill, Mr. Harris," said Davis with a smile, "and don't you worry. I'll see that he gets this story of his to a proper conclusion."

That's what I'm afraid of, thought Harris to himself.

IX

Las Vegas

March 2, 1977

Regan paced as Harris read the morning paper. They were waiting for Brad McCauley to bring Joe Paris up to Harris's room for the interview that McCauley had arranged the day before.

"Will you sit down?" said Harris.

"I think better on my feet," replied Regan.

"What're you doing? Trying to think up new ways to spend my money?"

Before Regan could come up with a sarcastic answer, there was a knock at the door. Regan rushed over to open it.

"How do you know your killer isn't out there?" asked Harris.

"You're right," said Regan as he turned away from the door. "You answer it."

"Who is it?" shouted Harris.

"Brad McCauley, Milt," came his answer.

"Let him in," said Harris to Regan.

Regan opened the door for McCauley who was accompanied by a man in a loud sportcoat. Regan assumed that he was looking at Joe Paris. He closed the door behind them as they made their way into the room. He watched Paris move like a cat toward the windows where he seated himself in a chair. Brad McCauley placed himself on the corner of the bed.

"Milt," said McCauley, "this is Joe Paris."

Harris reached over from his chair and shook hands with the dark-skinned man.

"Joe," said McCauley, "this is Tom Regan."

Regan stepped up to shake hands with Paris.

"So you're the guy who's digging into things that should be left alone," said Paris as he leaned back in the chair.

"That depends on your point of view," said Regan. "From where I stand, I see a crime that has never been solved properly. Where do you stand, Mr. Paris?"

"I stand alone," said Paris, "but I'm always looking over my shoulder to make sure someone isn't trying to sneak up on me."

"I don't think you have to worry about that, Mr. Paris," said Regan. "You're not the one I'm after."

"Then who are you after?"

"Mr. McCauley said you worked with anti-Castro Cubans in Florida back in the early sixties."

"That's right," said Paris. "I helped organize several guerrilla camps."

His English is too perfect, thought Regan.

"That's not exactly what I'm interested in, Mr. Paris," said Regan.

"Then what do you want to know," asked Paris as he smoothed his black hair with the fingers of his left hand.

"I want to know about some of the people you worked with."

"Anyone in particular?"

"Phil Schramm," said Regan as he watched the eyes of the little man for any signs of recognition of the name. There were none.

"I knew most of the CIA people who worked with my people," said Paris, "but I don't remember anyone by

113

that name."

Regan reached for the picture in his coat pocket. He handed it to Paris.

"Do you recognize that man?" asked Regan.

Paris studied the picture. He put his right index finger to his temple, as if it would induce him to recall the name of the man in the photograph.

"His face is familiar," said Paris slowly, "but I don't believe his name was Schramm." He continued to study the picture. "I think his name was Holman. Yes, that's it. Holman. Jimmy Holman. He taught my people how to use the M-1 rifle. He was a real marksman. He worked with two other fellows; a Williams and an Archer. Yes, Dave Williams and Paul Archer were their names. They were all better shots than they were teachers."

"Can you remember anything else about them?"

"Yes, I remember them very well," said Paris as he shifted his weight in the chair. "They were all from Texas, and they spoke Spanish as well as any Mexican, but not as well as a Cuban. Williams was a big man; maybe six foot two. He had black hair and was dark-skinned like a Mexican. He also had a very bad temper, and I remember someone saying he drank too much. The other man, Paul Archer, also had black hair, but he had very fair skin. He wasn't as tall as Williams. I'd say he was around six feet; maybe a little shorter. He was the nicest of the three. He treated my people with great respect. Holman looked much like he does in this picture. A little older perhaps but not much."

"How long did you know these men?"

"Let me see. I think they came to us in 1960. We were preparing to invade our homeland. All three men had received their training in the Marines, and they passed

114

that training onto my people. They were with us right up to the invasion. That was in April of 1961 if you remember. After that, we were forced to be more secretive about our operations; therefore, we moved our training camps to Louisiana. Archer, Williams, and Holman worked with us there for a year or so. When the FBI discovered our camps there, we all went separate directions. Some went to prison; others into exile in other countries; and I came here to Las Vegas. That was the last time I saw the three of them together."

"Then you've seen them separately since then?"

"Yes, I saw Archer and Williams in New Orleans in 1963 when I was there visiting my sister. We had a drink together in a little bar on Bourbon Street. I have since seen each one of them on several occasions here in Las Vegas, but not in the last two years or so."

"What about Holman?"

"I'm not sure about him," said Paris.

"What do you mean?" asked Regan.

"I took a fishing trip to Mexico last year, and I thought I saw him on the pier in Acapulco."

"What do you mean, you thought you saw him on the pier?"

"I saw a man who looked like him, but when I called to him, he made like he didn't even know me. I must have been mistaken, but at the time, I was so sure it was Holman. Before I could talk to him, he disappeared in the crowd."

"Hm-m, Mexico," muttered Regan as he stroked his beard. "Do you know if those were their real names?"

"No, I have no idea," said Paris.

"I might be able to help you there," said Brad McCauley. "I had a Dave Williams working for me in California at the same time that Oswald was there. He fits the description Joe gave of his Dave Williams."

"Now we're getting someplace," said Regan. "What do you think, Mr. Harris?"

"I'll call Phoenix and have someone check on those names with the Marines," said Harris. "If there's any records of Williams or the others, we'll find them."

"Is there anything else you can tell me about them, Mr. Paris?" asked Regan.

"No, that's about it."

"Thanks a lot, Mr. Paris. You've been very helpful."

"I still think you should leave anything to do with these men alone."

"What makes you say that?" asked Milt Harris.

"They are all killers," said Paris.

"How do you know that?" asked Regan.

"I can't tell you that," said Paris as he stood up to leave. "That is something I can't talk about now or ever."

"Why not?" asked Regan.

Paris smiled at him as he walked toward the door. He turned the doorknob and opened the door before turning to face Regan for the last time.

"I'm not going to tell you, Mr. Regan," said Paris, "and I hope you never find out. Do like I said; leave this thing alone."

"Not a chance," said Regan.

Paris was smiling as he closed the door behind him.

"Do you think he was making a threat, Brad?" asked Milt Harris.

"I don't think so," said McCauley. "Joe doesn't have the influence he thinks he has."

"What does that mean?" asked Regan.

"He thinks he has the Mafia eating out of his hand."

That sent a chill down Regan's spine.

"I wouldn't worry about Joe Paris. He's small potatoes, and murder isn't his bag."

"What is his bag?" asked Harris.

"Illegal aliens," said McCauley. "He gives them jobs when they get this far north."

"Why don't you turn him in?" asked Regan.

"He isn't my problem," said McCauley, "but the security of this hotel is, which means I have to get back to work. I'll see you gentlemen later."

McCauley was gone when Harris asked Regan what he planned to do next.

"Well, I think I'll go get Bill out of bed and head for the casino."

"I think I'll join you," said Harris.

They walked down to the eighth floor where they met Davis in the hall.

"I was just coming to look for you," said Davis. "You ran off again without me."

"If you didn't stay out so late," said Regan, "you wouldn't sleep in so late."

"Well, let me tell you about that," said Davis. "I ran into this little lady the other night who treated me real good, and she treated me real good last night, too. I can honestly say that she is one hundred proof woman."

"Ran up a little score, did you?" asked Regan with a big smile.

"I sure did," said Davis, "and what's more, she's got a couple of friends."

"What's it going to cost?" asked Harris.

"A dinner, a few drinks, and a lot of heavy breathing," laughed Davis.

"In that case," said Harris, "you can count me in."

"Then it's settled," said Regan. "Let's go get some

lunch.''

Davis took time out from lunch to call Lucy Hill, the girl he said he had met two nights before. He told her to bring her friends to the Four Queens anytime that day to meet his two friends. They would be in the casino playing blackjack.

Milt Harris took a few minutes away from the tables to call his right-hand man Gus Turner at *The Morning Sun* in Phoenix. He gave Gus the names of the three men Joe Paris had told Regan about, then ordered Gus to run a check on them with the Marines, the FBI, and as many police agencies as he could that afternoon. As soon as he had something, Gus was to call him back at the Four Queens and page him in the casino if there was no answer in his room.

A few minutes after six Harris heard his name announced over the public address system. He went to a house phone to answer the call. Regan went with him. As soon as he identified Gus Turner's voice, he told the operator to hold the call until he could take it in his room.

''Hello, Gus,'' said Harris when the connection was made to his room telephone. ''What did you find out about Archer, Williams, and Holman?''

''This took a lot of doing, boss,'' said Gus, ''but I managed to get a few things from the Marines. The FBI and the Dallas, New Orleans, and Phoenix police departments are still checking.''

''Okay, let's start with Archer,'' said Harris as Regan leaned close to him in order to hear Gus directly.

''Archer, Paul Austin. Born October 14, 1938 in Dalhart, Texas. Enlisted in the Marines January 1957. Served at Atsugi, Japan last two years of his enlistment. Discharged December 1959. According to his GI insurance, his last known address was a post office box in Scottsdale, Arizona.''

"Good job, Gus,'' said Harris. "Send someone over to Scottsdale and find out if the box is still in Archer's name. If it is, have someone keep an eye on it. I want pictures of everyone who takes mail from it.''

"Got it, boss.''

"Good. Who's next?''

"Williams, David Houston. Born June 12, 1937 in Corpus Christi, Texas. Enlisted in the Marines June of 1955. Served at Camp Pendleton, California last two years of his enlistment. Discharged in June 1960. Last known address was a post office box in Dallas, but that was seven years ago.''

"Not much to go on,'' said Harris, "but maybe the Dallas police will have something more on him. Go on with Holman.''

"Holman, James Alexander. Born May 28, 1937 in New Orleans. Enlisted in the Marines at Houston in June 1956. Served at Atsugi, Japan until May 1959. Transferred to Pensacola, Florida for remainder of enlistment. Discharged May 1960. Last known address was his mother's house in Youngtown, Arizona.''

"That's great work, Gus,'' said Harris. "Send someone out to Youngtown to see if Holman's mother still lives there, but be discreet about it. Don't let her know we're looking for her son. I'll handle that when I get home.''

"Right, boss. Anything else?''

"Not for now. I'll be coming in tomorrow morning. I'll call you from the airport.''

Harris ended the call.

"Now we're getting somewhere,'' said Harris.

"What do you mean 'we', white man?'' asked Regan.

"I thought this was my show."

"This thing is bigger than both of us, kid," said Harris. "Don't worry; you'll get the credit; but you have to admit that this is a job for more than one man."

"Okay, I'll admit that," said Regan, "but only as long as I get all the credit."

"You're going to need it," said Harris, "to feed that ego of yours."

"We can talk about this later. Right now, let's get back downstairs to Davis and those loose women who are supposed to be showing up soon."

They rejoined Davis in the casino at just the right time, because before they could pull their money out to play, Regan saw three nicely-built women approaching their table.

"Here come our bedwarmers now," said Davis as he also saw them.

"Hi, Bill," said the only blonde of the three as she put her arm around the big man's shoulders. "I'd like you to meet Bonnie and Faith."

The taller of the two brunettes nodded in Davis's direction. She was a real beauty, and the men took in as much of her as their eyes could behold. Besides her long brown hair, she had green eyes and plenty of curves in all the right places. The men did not have to undress her with their eyes; her see-through dress covered only the most important places.

The other dark-haired girl was not as pretty as her friends, but she was just as desirable. Her chestnut eyes spoke of something hot and wicked inside her. The light make-up on her nose and cheeks hid most of the freckles that made her look much younger than her obvious thirty years.

"It's nice to meet you, ladies," said Davis as he

turned on some of that charm that must have excited his ex-wife so much when she first met him. "I'd like you lovely young things to meet a couple of friends of mine from Phoenix. This is Tom behind the beard, and the distinguished-looking gentleman is Milt. Gents, meet Faith and Bonnie. I'd introduce you to Lucy here, but she belongs to me." Davis put his arm around Lucy's waist. "I guess you two'll have to fight or flip a coin over Faith and Bonnie."

"I don't think that will be necessary," said Bonnie as she seemed to glide over to Regan. "Beards really turn me on."

"Well, if I've got Faith, then I know there's hope," said Harris, "and maybe together we can find a little charity around here."

Regan was surprised at Harris. The old guy still had some pizzazz left in him.

"Well, all right, Milty," said Faith as she nuzzled up to Harris.

"Put it right here," said Harris as he patted the vacant chair next to him.

"Oh, good," said Faith as she slid into the seat. "Blackjack always turns me on."

Harris took a fifty from his wallet and pushed it toward the dealer.

"Give the lady some chips," he said.

Davis and Regan followed suit as they exchanged bills for five-dollar chips for their respective partners. Regan moved over to first base to make room for Lucy and Bonnie between him and Davis. Bonnie squeezed into the chair on Regan's left as Lucy made herself comfortable in the one that Davis had pulled out for her.

With introductions and basic small talk out of the way a half hour later, the three couples decided to go elsewhere for entertainment. Davis let Regan and Harris know that they were on their own as he and Lucy were off to take advantage of the privacy of her apartment. Regan and Harris took their women to a hotel on the Strip. Dinner, one show, and several drinks later, they returned to the Four Queens where Harris mentioned to Faith that it was time they went to find some charity. Regan took Bonnie to his room to make a similar search.

It did not take Bonnie more than the short walk from the door to the first double bed for her to slip out of her dress. Regan, who was not paying any attention to her, put the "Do Not Disturb" sign on the outside doorknob; closed the door; and latched it. Turning into the room, he flipped the switch that lighted the lamp between the beds. He took one step toward the beds but stopped when his eyes caught Bonnie's reflection in the mirror over the dresser. She was removing her last item of clothing, a pair of black silk bikini panties.

"How do I look?" she asked as she struck a pin-up pose for him. "I've been told that I belong in a magazine. What do you think?"

Regan was showing his thoughts with his eyes as his blood rushed to his extremities. He took two more steps toward her, and she met him halfway.

"What's the matter?" she asked as she removed his coat. "Cat got your tongue?" She unbuttoned his shirt. "I hope not."

Bonnie proved to be very adept at assisting him out of his clothes, then at leading him through the mazes of her body. She directed their mutual attack from the first assault of her mouth until the final clash of their hips.

They lingered in bed for breathless minutes before Bonnie nudged him aside. She moved to the other side of the bed and waited.

Regan was sated and near the edge of sleep. He hardly noticed Bonnie leaving the bed or the soft padding of her feet on the carpet as she went to the bathroom. A door slamming out in the hall jolted him back to cognizance. Slowly, he became aware of the sound of her fingers rustling through her purse as she stood naked in the bathroom. His eyes opened when she snapped the purse shut.

The lamp between the beds had been switched off during their love-making, leaving the room almost black. Only the light from the bathroom kept it from total darkness.

Regan looked toward the dresser mirror to see Bonnie's reflection from the bathroom. Her back was to him, but he was still enjoying the view. She was doing something with her hands, but he could not quite distinguish exactly what it was. He wondered if he had failed to satisfy her and if she was then doing something to find that satisfaction.

Then he saw it. His eyelids spread wide as they watched Bonnie fitting a silencer on the barrel of a .38 revolver.

Oh, shit, he thought, she's got a goddamned gun.

Although his heart was racing, he kept his head clear as he determined the action that he should take. He rolled out of the bed next to the wall that separated the room from the bath. He stood up inch by inch and moved to the corner next to the bathroom door. He could still see Bonnie's buttocks in the mirror, and that worried him because she might be able to see him standing there when she came out of the bathroom. He hoped the room was dark enough to keep her from seeing his reflection.

Bonnie had the gun ready. She stepped softly as she turned completely toward the bathroom doorway. She held the gun out away from her body as she stepped onto the carpet. She moved around the corner not knowing that Regan, who was holding his breath, was standing only three feet from her right arm, the one that held the gun. She took another step closer to the bed where she thought Regan was sleeping before raising the gun to a firing position.

It's too dark, she thought. I can't see him.

Another step toward the bed; she squinted her eyes to see the bed empty.

Regan was watching her eyes, those green cat's eyes that had turned him on when he had first looked into them.

Now, dummy, move! Regan could almost hear himself say as the air gushed from his lungs.

He grabbed the arm that held the gun with his right hand as he simultaneously threw his left arm around her throat. He nearly crushed her windpipe as he jerked his forearm against it. She gagged with the impact; she was caught by surprise. The air in her lungs tried to force itself free as she nearly panicked. She tried to whirl away from him by pounding her free elbow into his ribs, but he held on with all of his strength. Her feet stomped on his toes and kicked against his shins as he lifted her off the floor.

"Drop it!" he gritted through clenched teeth.

She gagged again as he jerked at her throat a second time. He continued to choke her into submission, if not death, as she fought back with flailing legs and a hand that reached up and grabbed his hair.

"Drop it, bitch!" he shouted into her ear.

She let the gun fall, but he continued to choke her as

she continued to fight for her life. He rocked backwards and fell on the other bed, pulling her down with him. He saw that her hand was free of the gun as he held it high above them. He released his stranglehold and pushed her off onto the floor. She scrambled for the gun as she gasped for air. Regan jumped to his feet next to her, quickly reaching down to grab her by the hair with his left hand. He jerked her to her knees. She reached for her throat, but her hands never got there as he landed a solid right fist to her face. Her arms dropped to her sides as she went unconscious. He withdrew his fingers from her hair and let her body fall to the floor. The gun was next to her, and he bent to pick it up.

With the gun securely in his possession, he found the light switch on the lamp and turned it on. He saw blood running from Bonnie's mouth and nose. She was breathing, which was all he wanted to know. He went to bathroom and soaked a towel in cold water. He washed away the blood and stopped her bleeding as he knelt beside her on the floor. Her face was already beginning to swell and discolor from his punch.

Regan left her laying there as he threw the gun into his suitcase and locked it before getting dressed. He made it a point to keep himself between her and the suitcase in case she should awaken before he was ready. She began to stir as he was tying his shoes. He reached over to shake her.

"Come on," he said, "wake up."

She groaned as the agony from her swelling face and bruised throat reached her brain. Her hands instinctively moved to the injured areas. She opened her eyes to see Regan standing over her. He bent to help her to the chair in the corner. She tried to speak, but her throat was too raw to make any sound. Regan looked at the mess he had made of her face. She was hardly pretty at that moment. She was still dazed when Regan threw her clothes at her.

"Get dressed!" he commanded.

She remained silent as she slowly slid into her clothes. Her eyes were glued to the floor as Regan paced the room.

"I want some answers," said Regan, "and I want them straight and fast."

"Go to hell!" she said hoarsely.

Regan slapped her across the face.

"Goddamn you!" she screamed as she found the power to speak more clearly.

"I said I wanted some answers."

Bonnie jumped up to attack him, but he only slapped her again knocking her back into the chair.

"Listen, you bitch," he said between clenched teeth, "somebody hired you to kill me, and I want to know who."

She remained silent.

He raised his hand to slap her a third time, but before he could bring it down, she whipped her foot up into his crotch. He doubled up from the pain, and she hit him in the face as hard as she could with both her hands clenched together. As he fell to one side, Bonnie bolted for the door. She was into the hall before Regan could regain enough strength to struggle after her. He crashed against the door as the pain in his testicles flared again. He grabbed his groin as he stumbled into the hall in time to see Bonnie rounding the corner to the elevators. He moved as fast as the pain would allow in pursuit of her. He heard the elevator doors open and close again before he could reach the corner. He turned the corner but stopped suddenly. Bonnie was on the floor in front of the elevators; her hands clutched at her chest trying to stop the flow of blood from her chest. Her eyes were wide with the disbelief that she had been shot, that she was dying.

"Tell me!" rasped Regan as he fell to his knees beside her.

Her lips tried to form the syllables of a name, but there was no sound. Regan clutched her by the shoulders as he lifted her head off the floor.

"Tell me!" he rasped again as he bent his ear to her lips.

Her head fell back as the sigh of death wheezed from her lungs. She was dead.

Regan eased her back to the floor and looked up at the numbers above the elevator doors. Bonnie's killer had gone straight down to the casino. He knew it would be senseless to pursue the murderer.

Now what? he wondered.

He wanted to run; he wanted to stay. Should he get help? Should he hide? What should he do?

Out of the confusion of his tumbling thoughts, he pulled the image of Milt Harris being murdered in the same way that Bonnie had intended to kill him.

"My God!" he gasped aloud.

There was no time to wait for the elevator, so he opted to take the stairs up to the ninth floor. With the pain in his groin lessening, he was able to move faster than he had when chasing Bonnie. He was still struggling as he moved down the hall of the ninth floor to Milt's door. He banged on it with his fist until he heard swearing from within. It was Milt cussing at the intruder at the door.

He's okay yet, thought Regan as he heard the door being unlatched.

Regan was using the door to prop himself up when Harris opened it. With his left hand still holding his painful groin, he kept himself from falling into the room by grabbing the doorjamb with his right hand.

"Regan!" said Harris as he stuck his head around the edge of the door.

Regan pushed the door open, forcing Harris back away from it. He stumbled into the room and closed the door behind him. He was breathing heavily as he noticed that the room was in total darkness. His hand felt for the light switch on the wall next to him. He found it, but only the night light at their feet came on when he flipped the switch.

"What's wrong, boy?" said Harris as he saw that Regan was having difficulty with his breathing and movements.

"Bonnie's dead," panted Regan.

"She's what?"

"Somebody shot her outside the eighth floor elevator," he went on, "but not till after she tried to kill me first."

"Bonnie tried to kill you?"

"You got it, Red Rider."

Faith was still in bed, but she was listening intently to their conversation. When she heard Regan say that Bonnie was dead, she knew that the time had come for her to make her move. She reasoned that if she killed both men she might be able to collect Bonnie's fee as well as her own.

Her gun was in her purse, which was on the chair in the corner. She had to get at it without being noticed. With stealthy movements, she slid out of bed between it and the window, creeping the few steps to the chair and watching Regan and Harris at the same time. Her right arm stretched out to retrieve the pocketbook, trying not to rattle any of its contents as she pulled it back against her naked torso. She shifted her eyes away from the two men as she fumbled for her gun and its silencer. As soon as she had them in her grasp, she carefully placed the purse on the end of the bed. Quickly now, Faith fitted the silencer to the gun; but as she neared the last turn, her car keys fell from her purse to the floor.

Regan heard the metallic thud of the keys hitting the floor, distracting him from his conversation with Harris. He stared into the darkness, faintly seeing Faith's silhouette against the drapes. She was doing something with her hands. The remembrance of Bonnie doing the same thing flashed through his brain.

"She's got a gun!" shouted Regan as he shoved Harris into the bathroom. He rushed toward Faith as she made the last turn of the silencer on the barrel of the .38.

She turned to fire at her attacker, but Regan was on her too quickly for her to get a clear shot. He grabbed her gun hand by the wrist; the pistol discharged its bullet into the wall. His momentum slammed her arm against the window behind her, causing the gun to fire again. Simultaneously, Regan threw his right forearm into her solar plexus smashing her against the window sill and snapping her head back against the glass. The .38 fell to the floor as the blow to her mid-section drove the air from her lungs and the collision of her head into the window shattered the glass. She bounced back against Regan; her arms and legs became limp as she was rendered unconscious.

Harris, who had lost his balance and slipped to one knee when Regan had pushed him into the bathroom, had come quickly to his feet. He jumped into the short hallway to see what was going on.

"What the hell are you doing?" he shouted at Regan as he turned on the lights that blinded both men for a few seconds and revealed the editor's nakedness.

Harris adjusted his vision in time to see Faith's body slide away from Regan as it slumped to the floor. Not seeing the gun that Regan was picking up, he rushed over to Faith.

"What have you done?" he demanded from Regan before looking up to see the writer twirling the gun around his index finger. His eyes were transfixed to the weapon as he realized that Regan had just saved their lives.

"My God, she was going to kill me!"

"You catch on quick," said Regan.

"But why?"

The tension of the moment escaped from Regan as he burst into laughter.

"What are you laughing at?"

"Take a look in the mirror," chuckled Regan.

Harris straightened up to go to the mirror, but then he caught on to Regan's warped sense of humor. Regan laughed all the harder as he saw the middle-aged editor's skin turn red from embarrassment.

"What's the matter?" growled Harris. "Haven't you ever seen a naked man before?"

Regan only roared harder as he watched Harris fumble for his clothes.

"Silly-assed punk kid," muttered Harris as he dressed. "I don't know why I ever hired you in the first place."

"I'm sorry, Milt," grinned Regan, "but I just realized how ridiculous you looked; and it was too much to hold back."

"All right, smart ass! Keep it up, and you'll find

yourself without a job.''

"You don't have to get sore," said Regan. "Just think how funny I'd look if I was in your place."

Harris began laughing as he imagined Regan in the same naked posture.

"I don't get it," said Harris, after the humor of their situation subsided.

"I'm not too sure I do either," said Regan as he regained his composure, "but it might be wise to call your friend McCauley and get him up here as soon as possible."

"You're right," said Harris as he dialed McCauley's private telephone number.

Regan kept a close eye on Faith as Harris talked with McCauley.

"Brad, this is Milt. I think you'd better come up to my room right away. There's been a murder."

"A murder?"

"Yes, on the eighth floor, but don't stop there. Come straight to my room. Regan and I are holding another girl here who tried to kill me."

"I'm on my way," said McCauley.

Regan revived Faith and gave her a blanket to cover herself with. He was not about to make the same mistake with her that he had with Bonnie. As long as she was naked, he reasoned, she would stay put.

"Have you got anything to say?" Harris asked her.

"Not to you," she sneered.

"You might be smart to talk to us," said Regan. "We're the only people who can help you now."

"That's what you think," said Faith.

"You can't count on Bonnie," said Regan. "She's dead, and that leaves only you."

"Shove it, you sonofabitch!"

131

"Suit yourself, lady."

Regan was still holding her gun as he sat on the end of the bed next to Harris.

"You know, Milt, now that I think about it, I don't remember any shots being fired when I was chasing Bonnie. Whoever killed her must've used a silencer, and that leads me to believe that he was waiting for her at the elevator."

"But how did he know she was coming just then?"

"Maybe he had followed us back to my room and was waiting for her to finish me off first."

"That's possible," said Harris. "The killer was probably there to make sure she killed you."

"Either that," said Regan as he watched Faith for any reaction from her, "or he was supposed to kill her all along."

Faith looked up at him startled by his revelation.

"That wasn't part of the deal," she said without thinking. "We were supposed to kill you two, then go collect our money."

"From who?" asked Harris.

Before she could answer, there was a knock at the door. Regan got up to answer it.

"Who's there?" he called out.

"Brad McCauley."

Regan opened the door, and McCauley rushed inside completely out of breath. He stared at the gun that Regan was still holding at his side.

"What the hell is going on here?" gasped McCauley. "What are you doing with that gun, and who is she?"

"The little lady in the corner is the owner of this little beast," said Regan as he held up the gun. "She was going to kill Milt with it."

"But Tom stopped her," said Harris.

"Thank God for that," said McCauley, "or I'd have two murders on my hands. What about the dead girl on the eighth floor?"

"She tried to kill me," said Regan.

"So he killed her instead," said Faith.

"I didn't kill her," said Regan.

"Then who did?" asked McCauley.

` I don't know. After I took her gun away from her, she kicked me in the balls and split. By the time I caught up with her, she was dying in front of the elevator. I didn't hear any shots, so her killer must've used a silencer on his gun. Then he took the elevator down to the casino."

"How do you know that?" asked McCauley.

"I watched the numbers above the elevator doors."

"Why was she trying to kill you in the first place?"

"I don't know," said Regan. "We were just about to get some answers out of her when you knocked at the door. Why don't we ask her?"

"I'm not talking any more," said Faith.

McCauley glared at her with those dark eyes of his. Faith looked away from them as she tried to escape their penetrating stare.

"I think you'd better talk," said McCauley in a low growl. "It might be healthier for you in the long run of things."

Faith knew what that meant.

"What do I get out of it if I do talk?" she bargained.

"I'll tell you what you're going to get if you don't," threatened McCauley.

Faith thought about it for a moment as she stared back at McCauley.

"It was Lucy's idea," said Faith.

"Lucy!" exclaimed Regan. "Holy shit, I forgot all about Bill and Lucy."

"Who are they?" asked McCauley.

"Bill is a friend of Tom's," said Harris, "and Lucy is a friend of hers. Bill met Lucy the other night and shacked up with her; then she set us up with her friends."

"What's Lucy's last name?" asked McCauley.

"Lucy Hill," said Faith. "She told us a guy who worked for Joe Paris hired her to kill all three of you. It seems that Joe Paris wants all of you dead."

"I can't believe Joe would do a thing like this," said McCauley. "Like I said before, murder isn't his style."

"I've got a hunch that you're right," said Regan. "I can't help thinking that there's someone else in this; someone who really feels threatened by what I've been digging up."

"Like who?" asked Harris.

"I only wish I knew," said Regan.

"I think it's time we let the police in on this," said McCauley. "I'm going down to the eighth floor to see what's going on down there."

McCauley left the room. Regan and Harris returned their attention to Faith as they waited for the police.

"Faith," said Regan, "is there anything else you can tell us about who hired you girls?"

"I've told you all I know," said Faith. "Lucy did all the talking for us. I never even saw the guy that hired us. All she said was this guy offered us five grand each to kill you guys. He said we could do it any way we wanted, just as long as it was done. Lucy thought up the plan to separate the three of you, and each one of us would kill the guy we were with. That's all there was to it."

"Only the guy who hired you had other ideas," said Harris. "He must've planned to kill all three of you

134

after you killed us."

"But how could he be in three places at once?" asked Regan.

"Maybe he had help," said Harris.

"It looks that way, doesn't it?" said Regan.

There was a knock at the door, and Regan got up to answer it. Two police detectives introduced themselves by displaying their badges. Regan permitted them to enter the room and introduced himself as well as Milt Harris and Faith.

The detectives began their questioning by having Regan and Harris tell them their versions of what had transpired that evening. After an hour of interrogation, the policemen officially arrested Faith, charging her with attempted murder. Their attempt to question her proved to be fruitless. Although she was willing to talk with Brad McCauley, she would say nothing to the police until she had consulted a lawyer. She knew what her legal rights were in a situation such as the one she was in. The policemen did permit her to dress in the bathroom before they departed with her for the police station.

"Lucy must've gotten Bill," said Regan after the police were gone.

"We don't know that for sure," said Harris.

"Then where is he?"

"The police will find him," said Harris. "Why don't you let them worry about Davis?"

"I suppose," said Regan. "I guess we may as well go to bed. I'll see you in the morning."

Regan took the stairs down to the eighth floor. As he passed the elevators where Bonnie had died, he saw a man shampooing the blood out of the carpet.

What a waste, he thought as he walked down the

corridor toward his room. A girl with her looks could have done a lot better.

He opened the door and turned on the light. The light went out again immediately after someone near the lamp between the beds switched it off.

"Close that door," whispered Bill Davis.

"Bill!" cried Regan.

"Shut up and close the door!"

Regan obeyed. The light came back on as soon as Davis heard the door being locked.

"Are you all right?" asked Regan.

"Of course, I am," said Davis who was sitting on the bed next to the window, a gun resting on the pillow. "How about you?"

"I managed to escape," said Regan as he sat down on the other bed. "Where have you been?"

"It's a long story, Tom, but I'll make it as short as possible."

"Okay, shoot," said Regan before he remembered the gun on the pillow. "I mean. . ."

"I know what you mean," snapped Davis. "Sorry about that. I get kind of edgy when someone tries to kill me."

"Then Lucy tried to kill you, too?"

"Yeah, she tried, but she'll never try again." Davis paused as he waited for Regan's reaction. "I killed her."

"You what?"

"That little bitch pulled a gun on me. When I went to take it away from her, it went off. That bullet sure made a mess out of her right tit. It must've gone right through her heart because she was dead before she hit the floor."

"Then it was self-defense," said Regan. "I think we

136

can convince the police of that."

"I can't go to the police, Tom."

"But you have to."

"I can't; I'm wanted in Texas on a drug charge. If the police here check on me, I'll go straight back to Texas and prison."

"What drug charge?"

"I used to be small-time pusher while I was going to school in Dallas. I got busted for it, but I jumped bail. They had me dead to rights. I didn't have any other choice if I wanted to stay out of prison."

"What happens when they find Lucy's body? They're going to find your fingerprints all over the apartment. They'll come after you and me, too, for harboring a fugitive from justice. What then, Bill?"

"They aren't going to find her body," said Davis. "I put it where no one's going to find it."

"Don't tell me," said Regan. "I don't want to know where it is."

"I wasn't going to anyway. If I was to tell you, I'd never feel safe."

"I see your point," said Regan. "Okay, we'll play it your way, but I'll have to tell Milt Harris about this."

"No, you don't," snapped Davis. "I mean, what he don't know can't hurt him or me either. Let's just get our things together and get the hell out of this town."

"In the morning," said Regan. "I have to take Milt to the airport. Besides, it would look too suspicious if we leave tonight."

"You're right; we'll leave in the morning for California."

How did he know we were going to California? wondered Regan. I didn't tell him that.

He fell asleep with that thought still worrying him.

X

Garden Grove, California

March 3, 1977

The morning had come and gone. Regan had taken Milt
Harris to the airport while Bill Davis remained hidden in
their room. Regan had not divulged to Harris that Davis
was alive and well. The editor had boarded his plane
still thinking that Davis was dead. Regan, after promising to call Harris as soon as he arrived at a motel in
Garden Grove, had returned to the Four Queens to get
Davis. Regan had checked out while Davis had taken
the back stairs out of the hotel. They had met at Regan's
car in the parking building. They had wasted no time in
getting out of Las Vegas.

The distance between the Nevada city and their destination was about 250 miles. The traffic on the highway
was negligible as they crossed the empty desert. They
defeated the boredom of the tedious trip by discussing
the events of the past month as they had happened to
Regan.

Outwardly, Regan was relaxed and comfortable as he
narrated his findings to Davis. Behind his calm aspect,
he was hiding the growing anxiety that his life was in
greater danger than it had ever been before. Caution
was the watchword that nagged at him.

Davis gave the impression that he was hanging on
every word as he listened. He asked pertinent questions
at the appropriate intervals in Regan's dialogue. His

138

inquiries stimulated Regan's memory. Not until Regan finished with the events of the night before did Davis ask the one question that troubled him the most.

"Have you got any idea who might be trying to kill you, Tom?"

"That's just it," shrugged Regan. "I haven't got the slightest idea who the killer is. I can believe that Joe Paris was behind the girls in Vegas, but what about the other attempts? Who killed that kid up in Oregon? Who killed Hewitt in Salt Lake? Paris couldn't have known about me then; at least, I don't think he could've known. No, someone else committed those murders; probably someone who knew Hewitt; someone who knew about his book and that list of people that had known Oswald; someone who was afraid Hewitt would find out something he wasn't supposed to. Whoever that person is probably killed Paul Bagdonovich back in December."

"Why would anyone want to kill Paul Bagdonovich two months before you started investigating this?"

"It beats the hell out of me. Hewitt denied ever having called Bagdonovich. If he was telling the truth, then someone knew about his book back then. Hewitt did tell Mrs. Bagdonovich that Paul may have been the last link between Oswald and Schramm."

Regan realized that he had struck the right key at last.

"That's it," exclaimed Regan. "Bagdonovich and Schramm. That's the connection. That's why he was killed; he knew something that could connect Oswald and Schramm, alias Jimmy Holman."

"Like what?" queried Davis.

"I don't know," said Regan, "but as soon as we're through with Cortland, we're heading for Phoenix to see Rita Bagdonovich."

139

"Do you think she might hold the key to all this?"

"I don't know for sure, but I've got a hunch she does. She has to. Why else would Hewitt tell her that her husband was the last link between Oswald and Schramm?"

Davis did not answer. He appeared to be concentrating on his driving as they were coming down from the high desert into the San Bernadino Valley through Cajon Pass. He continued to be quiet as the traffic began increasing outside San Bernadino. Regan thought it best not to disturb him until they reached their motel in Garden Grove.

Brad McCauley had prepared the way for Regan by calling ahead. He had informed Jack Cortland that Regan was a friend who was trying to right some of the wrongs done so many years before. Cortland had been cautious but cooperative. He had told McCauley that as long as Regan stuck to the question of his relationship with Oswald, he would provide all the information he knew. Regan had agreed with Cortland's demand.

Davis drove Regan's car from the Garden Grove Freeway onto Harbor Boulevard. They travelled north on Harbor until they reached the Fantasyland Motel which was across from Disneyland. Since it was the off-season for the tourist trade, they had no difficulty in getting a room. It was late in the afternoon when Regan sat down to call Jack Cortland.

"Cortland's," answered a strong male voice.

"Mr. Cortland?" said Regan.

"Speaking."

"Mr. Cortland, this is Tom Regan. I believe Brad McCauley phoned you about me."

"Yes, Mr. Regan, he did," said Cortland, "but that was before those murders in Las Vegas."

"Does that mean you're not willing to talk to me now?" asked Regan.

"Let's just say I think it might be unhealthy for me if I did."

"Has somebody threatened your life?"

"No, but I'm not going to take any chances either. I quit the Bureau because I didn't want any more danger in my life' and I haven't changed that attitude over the years."

"I wish you would reconsider," said Regan. "I feel that the information you have will be quite beneficial to my story."

"I'm sure it would be," said Cortland, "but unless you can guarantee my safety, we might as well stop talking right now."

"I can't do that," regretted Regan. "Couldn't I come over to your house and discuss this with you?"

"Absolutely not," said Cortland. "That would be the worst possible thing you could do."

"Well, couldn't we meet here in my motel room?"

"That's out of the question, too."

"Well, could you tell me what you know over the phone?" asked Regan.

"That would only be hearsay, Mr. Regan. A telephone conversation with a man you have never met before is not admissable evidence."

"Then could we meet in a public place where there would be a large number of people around?"

"That sounds reasonable."

"I'm not familiar with this area, so you'll have to suggest the place."

"Okay, I'll meet you at Disneyland."

"Disneyland?" asked Regan.

"That's right," said Cortland. "The place will be

fairly crowded. I don't think anyone will try anything there."

"Okay, where do you want me to go and how will I know you?"

"No, Mr. Regan, you tell me how I'll find you and what you look like."

"I've never been to Disneyland," said Regan.

"Okay, listen closely," said Cortland. "You go through the gate, then through one of the tunnels into the town square. Walk down Main Street toward Sleeping Beauty's Castle. Go straight to the castle. There's a moat just in front of the castle with a bridge over it. I'll meet you there at six o'clock. Now tell me what you'll be wearing."

"I'll be wearing a pale green sport coat," said Regan. "I've got a beard and fairly shaggy hair. The beard has streaks of white in it around my chin, but my hair is all brown. Anything else?"

"That should be sufficient," said Cortland. "I'll see you at six."

Cortland hung up.

"Well, what's the score?" asked Davis.

"I'm going to meet him at Disneyland at six," said Regan as replaced the receiver.

"That's less than two hours away," said Davis. "It smells to me."

"I don't have any other choice."

"Well, I'd better come along just to make sure this guy doesn't have something up his sleeve."

"I don't think that will be necessary," said Regan. "Besides, you might scare him off."

"I could keep a safe distance," said Davis.

"No, I can't risk it. Just stay here; I'll be all right. Disneyland is probably about as safe a place as any. I

142

don't think anyone would try to commit murder with so many people around.''

"I guess you're right," said David. "I think I'll go get a drink. Feel like coming along?"

"No," said Regan, "You go ahead. I've got to call Milt Harris in Phoenix."

"You going over to Disneyland after that?"

"Probably."

"Then I guess I won't see you till later this evening," said Davis. "Be careful, Tom. I still don't like the smell of this."

"Go get your drink," said Regan.

Davis was still shaking his head as he left the room. Regan felt reassured by his concern; he was almost touched by it.

Milt Harris was just leaving his office when Regan's call came. The editor returned to his desk to answer it.

"Where are you staying, Tom?"

"I'm at the Fantasyland across from Disneyland," said Regan.

"Got it," said Harris as he wrote down the name of the motel. "Don't stray too far from there. I may want to call you this evening."

"Are you expecting something to happen that I should know about?"

"Yeah, I'm going over to see Holman's mother later tonight. If she has anything that you might need before you get back here tomorrow, I'll call you about it. In the meantime, I received a call from Brad McCauley this afternoon. They found Joe Paris."

"Did he talk?" asked Regan.

"No, someone had fixed him so he couldn't; his throat was cut. They found his body in a mine shaft near

143

Searchlight. He'd been dead since yesterday evening. They found his car parked downtown this morning. There was blood all over the trunk. Someone slit his throat, stuffed him into the trunk, then drove him out to the mine where they found his body. The police figure he died between eight and nine last night. That wasn't more than ten hours after he talked to us.''

''Doesn't that cast a little doubt on Faith's story about Paris hiring her and her friends?''

''It would seem so,'' said Harris, ''but she's sticking to it. She told the police that Paris hired them yesterday morning through some guy that she never met. The go-between only talked with Lucy Hill, but the police haven't found her yet.''

And they probably won't for a long time, thought Regan.

''I'm beginning to doubt that Paris had anything to do with those girls.''

''There's more, Tom. The Vegas police ran a check on Paris's fingerprints, and they found out that his real name is Jose Perez from Havana, Cuba. He was wanted by the FBI for some anti-Castro activities he had a part in back in the early sixties. The last lead they had on him was in Dallas in November of '63.''

''This thing is really starting to heat up,'' said Regan. ''Maybe Jack Cortland can add something to our information on Paris.''

''That's what I was thinking,'' said Harris.

''Have you learned anything more about Holman, Archer, or Williams?''

''I was just coming to that. The Vegas police found a lot of prints in Lucy Hill's apartment. So far, they have only been able to identify two sets. One belongs to Lucy, of course; but the other, interestingly enough,

144

belongs to David Williams.''

"Williams!'' exclaimed Regan.

"That's right,'' said Harris. "They only found a thumbprint and an index finger impression, but they were enough. It looks like Williams is your killer.''

"I wish you'd put that a different way,'' said Regan. "I'm not exactly dead yet.''

"Well, you'd better watch yourself. This Williams could be anyone. The information the Vegas police got said he was a master of disguises.''

"Don't lose any hair over me,'' said Regan. "I can take care of myself.''

"Yeah, sure,'' said Harris. "I don't want to print this story of yours posthumously, so be careful.''

"I said not to worry.''

"Okay, I won't,'' said Harris. "I'll see you in my office tomorrow.''

"Yeah, right,'' said Regan, and the conversation came to a conclusion.

Regan looked at his watch to see that it was almost five o'clock. He wondered if he should leave for Disneyland right then. He looked around the room to see a pamphlet with information on the area surrounding the motel. He perused it to find that a shuttle bus came by the motel every half hour to take tourists to and from Disneyland. It came by the Fantasyland at a quarter after and a quarter before every hour. He decided to take the five-fifteen over to the park.

It was five-thirty when Regan walked through the tunnel that went under the Disneyland railroad station. As he walked through the town square, he was amazed by the number of people there. Gazing at the shops, the horsedrawn trolley car as it passed, and the costumed employees of the park, he was nearly caught up in the fairytale atmosphere which invited everyone to forget the turmoil of the outside world. But he knew he had a job to do first.

It was a few minutes before six when he paused on the drawbridge to the castle to gaze at two white swans that swam in the water below.

"Beautiful creatures, aren't they?" said a man's voice next to him.

Regan glanced to his right to see a heavy-set man leaning on the railing next to him. He was also enjoying the serenity of the swans.

"It's a damned shame," continued the middle-aged gentleman in the navy blue cardigan, "that the whole world can't be as peaceful as this place."

"I know what you mean," said Regan as he turned to face Jack Cortland.

"Mr. Regan, I presume," said Cortland as he also turned to face Regan, standing erect to his full height of six feet two.

"It's a pleasure to meet you, Mr. Cortland," said Regan as he held out his hand to accept Cortland's handshake.

"Since this is your first visit to Disneyland, Mr. Regan, permit me to show you the best view of the park."

"Lead the way," said Regan.

Cortland lumbered off the bridge toward Tomorrowland, and Regan kept pace at his side. As they ambled through the crowd, Cortland pointed to the attractions as they passed them, adding bits of information about each one. They came up to a ramp that led up to the Skyway to Fantasyland. Cortland handed Regan a ticket for the ride in the open tramway cars that passed over the center of Disneyland. They went up the ramp with Cortland still talking about the exhibits and other

146

rides that surrounded them. They handed their tickets to a young girl in a futuristic costume before entering the tramway car.

"Now to get down to business," said Cortland as soon as they were out over the park. "I chose this ride because no one will be able to see me hand this."

Cortland reached inside his sweater and pulled out a large white envelope. He made it a point to keep it below the rim of the car as he handed it to Regan.

"What's in it?" asked Regan.

"Photocopies of several documents that were supposedly destroyed in 1963 and '64. All of them prove that Lee Harvey Oswald was a government agent working for both the CIA and FBI."

"Where are the originals?" asked Regan.

"I have them locked up in a safe place," said Cortland. "Until this moment, I have been the only person on this earth that knows that those documents still exist. Now you know, too."

Regan turned the envelope over to see that it was sealed. He started to open it, but Cortland reached over and grabbed his hand.

"Don't open it here," said Cortland. "Just put it inside your coat for now. Open it someplace where you can be alone."

"All right," said Regan. He placed the envelope inside his coat. "Now tell me about Oswald. Did he work for you like Brad McCauley said?"

"Yes, Oswald worked for me as an informant. He approached me in the spring of '63 on Brad McCauley's recommendation. I checked him out and found out that he had worked with the CIA for almost four years. I hired him as a contract informant. We only paid him for the information he delivered."

"Exactly what kind of information was he gathering for you?"

"At that time, we were trying to locate anti-Castro Cubans who were running an illegal guerrilla training camp in the New Orleans office. It was Oswald's job to find these people and their camp."

"Did he find anything?" asked Regan.

"He certainly did," said Cortland just as their car passed through the Matterhorn. "He was really good at getting all kinds of information. I knew he was under contract to the CIA, and I always supposed that he was getting most of his dope from them."

"I read in a book that Oswald may have sent your office a message a few days before the assassination in Dallas warning you of the plot to kill the President. Is there any truth in that?"

"There's a copy of that letter in the envelope," said Cortland. "You can read the whole thing later, but I'll give you the gist of it now. That message came in on the seventeenth of November, five days before the President was killed. As soon as I was notified of it, I put all of my agents on alert. I then sent a copy of the message on to Washington. Two days later, I was notified by the big man himself to disregard the warning as a false alarm. Oswald hadn't steered me wrong yet, but I obeyed the directive."

"Did you have any contacts with Oswald after that?"

"No, that was the last time I heard from him."

Their car arrived at the Fantasyland station. Instead of disembarking, Cortland handed the attendant two more tickets for the return trip to Tomorrowland.

"If someone was following us," said Cortland, "he'll be dog-tired by the time he gets back to Tomorrowland."

Regan waited for their car to clear the station before renewing his questioning.

"McCauley said that you quit the Bureau because of the way the assassination investigation was conducted. Is that true?"

"Yes, that's why I quit," said Cortland as he took a pack of cigarettes from his shirt pocket. "People in high places seemed to be doing everything in their power to suppress every piece of evidence that led away from Oswald. It seemed to me that they wanted him to be guilty just because he was dead."

Cortland took a lighter from his pants pocket and lit the cigarette he had taken from the pack that he had put back into his shirt pocket. He dragged deeply on the tobacco as he replaced the lighter. He exhaled before continuing.

"Most of what you'll need is in that envelope. I could tell you a lot of other things, but they won't do you any good in a court of law."

"I'm mostly interested in finding out if Oswald had a double who might have been mixed up in the conspiracy to kill the President. Do you know anything about that?"

"I've heard that theory," said Cortland. "I recall that there were some rumors that Oswald or someone who looked a lot like him was seen in Phoenix, Arizona a week after the assassination, but we were told not to check it out because Oswald was dead."

"Have you ever heard of Jose Perez?" asked Regan.

"Yeah, I remember him. He ran the camp we found near Lake Ponchartrain in '63. We never caught him. It was a tip from Oswald that led us to that camp."

"Okay, how about a man named James Alexander Holman? Have you ever heard of him?"

"You mean James Alek Hidell, don't you?"

"Hidell? No, I said Holman."

"Yeah, I know that was his real name, but he went by the alias of James Alek Hidell most of the time."

"I thought Oswald used that alias," said Regan.

"That's part of the information that was twisted to suit the needs of the Warren Commission."

"But Oswald had that name on some piece of ID when he was caught in Dallas."

"No, that's what the Dallas police said he had on him after the FBI found out about the post office box where a certain rifle was sent earlier that year. In order to prove that Oswald was the holder of the box, he had to have the alias of Hidell. That would tie him to the rifle, which in turn would tie him to the assassination."

"You mean Oswald didn't have any ID with that name?"

"I didn't say that because I don't know that for certain. All I'm saying is that the Dallas police made no mention of it until after the Bureau told them about the post office box and the rifle."

"What else do you know about Holman?" asked Regan as they were inside the Matterhorn.

"I know that he was working for the CIA out of the New Orleans office and that he was involved in training Cuban guerrillas."

"How about a guy named Paul Archer? Have you ever heard of him?"

"He was with the CIA, too," said Cortland. "He worked with Holman and a man named David Williams. We found out that the three of them were training guerrillas for Perez. We never caught any of them."

Regan took the picture of Holman, alias Schramm, alias Hidell, from his inside coat pocket. He handed it

150

over to Cortland who inspected it closely.

"Do you know that man?" asked Regan.

"That all depends," said Cortland, "on when this picture was taken. If it was taken before Oswald got that scar on the left side of his head, then I'd say it was him. On the other, if it was taken after that, it could be anyone who bears a strong resemblance to him."

"That man is James Holman," said Regan. "My brother-in-law took that picture, but he knew him as Phil Schramm."

"Schramm?"

"Yeah, does it mean something to you?"

"I'm not sure," said Cortland before taking a drag on his cigarette. He was pensive for a moment, then he said, "Now I remember. That was the name of a man whose boat I chartered in Ensenada a few years ago. That's strange. Now that I think about it, I remember thinking then that he looked a lot like Oswald even with his long hair and beard and Spanish accent. It was his eyes that made me think that."

"What was the name of that place again?" asked Regan.

"Ensenada," said Cortland. "It's a fishing resort south of Tijuana. I go down there once a year to go deep sea fishing. I only saw this guy the one time, but I'm sure his name was Phil Schramm."

Regan was busy writing the name of the town in his pocket notebook as their car arrived at the Tomorrow-land station. He expected Cortland to hand the attendant two more tickets, but the big man disembarked instead. Regan followed him out onto the platform. He started to ask Cortland another question, but before he could, Cortland was moving away from him.

"How did you like the view from up there?" asked

151

Cortland when Regan was alongside him again.

"Very impressive," said Regan as he sensed that Cortland did not want to talk about Oswald anymore.

"I thought you might enjoy it," said Cortland. "Have you had supper yet?"

"No, not yet," said Regan.

"Well, I was thinking about having dinner here in the park," said Cortland. "Would you care to join me?"

"Certainly," said Regan as they walked down the ramp to ground level.

Neither man said anything until they were seated in one of the outdoor restaurants with their food in front of them.

"Mr. Cortland, may we continue our discussion?"

"Certainly."

"Good, because I've still got a lot of questions to ask you."

"For instance?"

"You said Oswald had a scar on the left side of his head. No one else told me that."

"Maybe that's because they weren't trained to notice things like that."

"What about Archer and Williams? Can you remember what they looked like?"

"No, I can't help you there," said Cortland. "I never saw any of them."

"Do you know if those three men were part of the conspiracy to kill the President?"

Cortland chewed and swallowed a bite of chicken; then he wiped his mouth with a paper napkin before answering the question.

"In January of '64, I leaked information about Oswald's connection to the Bureau to some very important people who I thought would make it public. The info was never formally made known to the public. On the last day of January that year, I received another order from Washington. In so many words, I was told to instruct my agents not to follow up on any leads that would connect Oswald to the Bureau or the CIA. Attached to that directive was a list of people we were not to question nor even contact. On that list were the names of every known CIA and Bureau agent in the South, including those of Holman, Archer, and Williams. That was when I decided to quit the Bureau.''

"Why didn't you do something about the coverup back then?" asked Regan.

"I'm a married man, Mr. Regan," said Cortland. "I have five children, only one of which was grown up at that time. I wanted to live to see her graduate from college as well as see the rest of my kids grown up. People who knew too much were already dying mysteriously. I wasn't about to go showing those papers to the whole world back then.''

"I guess I can't blame you for looking out for yourself," said Regan. "I've already had a few attempts made on my life this past month since I started delving into this thing.''

Cortland was looking around at the surrounding tables. He gave Regan the impression that he was dissatisfied with something.

"Is something wrong?" asked Regan.

"Yeah, I don't like the location of this table," said Cortland. "Let's move over to that one by the wall.''

"If you insist," said Regan.

"I insist," said Cortland as he picked up his tray and started for the empty table.

Regan followed him, and both men placed their trays on the table at the same time. They sat down and resumed their meal.

"You said there were some attempts on your life, Mr. Regan," said Cortland. "I hope the man who's after you doesn't show up here. A lot of innocent people could get hurt."

Cortland opened his sweater just enough for Regan to see the shoulder holster under his left arm.

"I still carry the thing," said Cortland as if he disapproved of violence and guns. "Do you see any salt on this table?"

"No, I don't," said Regan.

"I don't either," said Cortland as he turned to ask a lady at the table next to them if he could borrow the shaker from her table.

Regan was just taking a bite out of a chicken thigh when the bullet smashed into the wall next to Cortland's head. It would have killed the former FBI agent if he had not turned around so suddenly. Regan dropped the piece of chicken and pushed himself away from the table upsetting it as he did. He dropped to the floor immediately.

Cortland felt chips of plaster biting into his neck just as he heard the thud of the bullet. He turned back around in time to catch a lap full of chicken and french fried potatoes. He saw Regan going to the floor, as he wasted no time in joining him there. As he was ducking, Cortland pulled his Smith and Wesson from its shoulder holster. He kept it hidden from the views of the other patrons in the restaurant as he held the gun against his chest under his sweater. With trained eyes, he looked around for his would-be assassin.

The lady at the next table heard the same thumping noise of the bullet hitting the plaster wall as Cortland had heard. She, however, had no idea what had caused the sound. All she saw was a strange man prostrate on the floor and a second man with his dinner in his lap going down to join the first. She thought they were crazy at first; then knowing that Disneyland was full of surprises, she concluded that they were part of an act that was going to give a show for everyone in the restaurant.

The other diners, nearly fifty of them, assumed the same two conclusions. Instead of screaming and running for cover, they waited patiently at their tables for the next piece of action. They were a hushed audience anticipating some real live entertainment.

Cortland and Regan scanned the restaurant first in an effort to recognize their assailant, but no one appeared to be of a suspicious nature. Their eyes went to the people strolling past the restaurant. Everything seemed normal there. They looked beyond the street to the little plaza that was the center of Disneyland.

"There he is," whispered Regan. "The tall man with the camera aimed right at us."

"I see him," said Cortland. "Stay low, and try to act like nothing's wrong."

"Who are you kidding?" grunted Regan.

The man with the camera was on the move. He joined the pedestrians in the street. He was walking quickly toward the park entrance.

"He's running," said Cortland as he jumped to his feet. "Come on; let's get him."

Cortland dashed through the restaurant bumping into tables, chairs, and other diners as he went. Regan followed him, but being much smaller in stature, he agilely avoided colliding with any of the objects or people that dogged Cortland's path. They were in the street skipping through the crowd as fast as they could. The man with the camera was already in the tunnel under the railroad station when Cortland and Regan entered the town square. By the time they were through the tunnel, their quarry was through the gate and into the parking lot. Cortland was near exhaustion when he pushed his way through the turnstile. Regan still had plenty of vigor left in him as he passed Cortland in the parking lot.

"What are you doing?" heaved Cortland. "You don't have a gun."

Regan did not hear him, but the Disneyland security officers who were pursuing them did. Two uniformed men came up behind Cortland on the run just as he pulled his gun from inside his sweater. Cortland raised it to take a shot at the fleeing man, but the security men grabbed his arms, spoiling his aim. The gun discharged into the asphalt.

The shot rang in Regan's ears, but he kept running after the tall man who had aimed his camera at them. He was closing in on his prey as they both passed beneath the high voltage towers that divided the parking area in halves. The man with the camera looked back over his shoulder to see Regan a few steps behind him. A station-wagon heading for the exit was directly in his path. He made for it. Regan failed to notice the vehicle as he was concentrating on the chase.

"Look out, Charlie!" screamed the lady passenger in the station-wagon when he saw the tall man running at their car.

The driver stomped his foot on the brake stopping the car. The tall man leaped onto the hood, then over to the other side. Regan, who was just about to tackle the man, crashed into the fender knocking the wind out of himself. He collapsed on the ground as his assailant fled to safety.

"Oh, my God, Charlie!" screamed the lady passenger again. "You hit him!"

"The hell I did!" said Charlie as he jumped out of his car and rushed around to where Regan lay gasping for breath. "What the hell's the idea of running to my car like that? What are you? Some kind of nut or something? I always thought these Californians were a bit strange."

"Shut up, Charlie!" snapped the lady as she climbed out of the car. "Can't you see he's hurt."

"Serves the bastard right, running into my car like that," said Charlie.

By this time, a crowd was beginning to gather. The two security officers came to the forefront with Cortland between them. One officer held Cortland's gun, while the other knelt down to check on Regan.

"Are you all right, buddy?" asked the officer.

"I'll live," panted Regan.

"Lucky for you," said the officer, "we grabbed this guy before he could get a shot off."

Regan stared up at Cortland who was shaking his head as if to say that he should go along with the officer's assumption.

"Yeah, damned lucky," said Regan as he regained his breath and came to his feet.

"What was he after you for?" asked the officer.

"I think it was a case of mistaken identity," said Regan.

"That's right," said Cortland hastily. "I thought he was a criminal that we were after."

"What are you talking about?" asked the officer.

"I'm with the FBI," said Cortland. "If you'll look in my wallet, you'll find my identification."

The officer holding his gun removed Cortland's wallet from his right rear pants pocket. He went through the wallet carefully to find an ID card with Cortland's picture on it.

"He's telling the truth, Ted," said the officer. "He is an FBI agent."

"Gee, we're sorry for interfering, sir," said Ted.

"It's a good thing you did," said Cortland. "I might've shot an innocent man if you hadn't."

"Who were you after?" asked Regan. "I'd like to know who the crook is that I look like."

"Well, son," said Cortland, "if you'll let me buy you a cup of coffee or even dinner as a form of apology, I'd be glad to tell you all about it."

"My mama told me never to turn down a free meal," said Regan. "I accept."

"Fine," said Cortland. "If I could have my gun back, officer, this young man and I will be on our way."

The security officer returned Cortland's .38 to him without saying anything, but his partner was already attempting to disperse the crowd.

"My car's right over here," said Cortland as he led Regan away from the scene.

Neither of them looked back at the security police or the onlookers until they were safely in the car.

"That was fast thinking back there," said Cortland. "We'd both be in a lot of trouble if they had hauled us in to the police. The Anaheim P.D. doesn't appreciate it when people disturb their tourists, especially when it happens at Disneyland."

"I think I know what you mean," said Regan. "How come you still have an FBI ID card on you?"

"I'm a retired agent," said Cortland. "Fortunately, that security cop didn't take the card out and turn it over to see that it was stamped retired."

"I guess we both did some fast talking," said Regan.

"Yes, we did," said Cortland. "Where are you staying? I'll drop you at your hotel."

"The Fantasyland."

"That's appropriate," said Cortland as he maneuvered his car through the traffic.

"Well, don't lose any sleep over this, Mr. Cortland. Not yet, anyway. I've still got a few more leads to track down before I'll be asking you to come forward to verify everything with those original documents."

"I wish you a lot of luck," said Cortland as he pulled his car into the driveway of the motel. "You've had plenty up to now, but how long will it last?"

Regan climbed out of the car. He turned to say his reply to Cortland's question, but the former FBI agent drove away too soon. He was gone before Regan could even thank him or say good-bye, but his last words haunted Regan the rest of the week.

XI

Phoenix

March 4, 1977

Milt Harris was in the middle of a meeting with his staff of editors when Regan walked into his office unannounced. The meeting room was adjacent to Harris's private office, but the managing editor of *The Morning Sun* could still see anyone who entered his personal domain from where he sat at the editors' conference table. As soon as he saw Regan walk through the door he wrapped up the meeting as quickly as possible.

"Well continue this on Monday," said Harris to his staff. "I would appreciate all of you devoting a little time to the special feature we discussed earlier. I have a feeling that we'll be running it in the very near future. I want it covered from all angles, including the women's section."

There were a few murmurs from the staff and a cough or two as they shot disagreeable looks in every direction but that of Milt Harris. This was their customary reaction to being given weekend assignments by the boss. They were much like a classroom of kids who had been given a weekend homework assignment.

"That will be all," said Harris. "I want each of you in here by eight o'clock Monday morning."

Each one of them rolled his or her chair away from the table, and in pairs or small groups, they left the conference room by the door that led into the hall instead of the one to Milt's office. As soon as they had all gone, Harris stood up.

"It's about time you showed up," said Milt as he shuffled some papers in front of him.

"You seem to have things under control here," said Regan from the doorway to the meeting room. "I never realized that you were a Captain Bligh."

"What makes you think that?"

"There's rumblings of mutiny from the crew," said Regan. "Your people don't seem to appreciate what you're doing for them."

"How observant of you," said Harris as he moved toward his private office. "I'm not worried about it though."

"Oh, yeah?" snorted Regan. "Why not?"

"The publisher and I are related by marriage," said Harris as he slid past Regan through the doorway. "None of those people can say that."

"I didn't know that," said Regan. "Is that why you can act so high and mighty around here?"

"How would you know that?" snapped Harris. "You've only been here once before."

"Sensitive today, aren't we?"

"Now look here, Regan; it's time we got something straight. I run this newspaper, not you or anyone else for that matter. I don't need any bullshit from you about how I do it. Is that understood?"

"For a guy whose life I saved, you don't appear to be very grateful."

"I knew it," said Harris as he rolled his eyes. "I knew it. I knew you'd remind me of that."

"And why shouldn't I? How would you feel if you were in my shoes?"

"Okay, okay," Harris surrendered. "You saved my

161

life, but what have you done for me today?"

"Is that the prevailing attitude around here?"

"That is the prevailing attitude everywhere," said Harris.

"Not with me, it isn't," challenged Regan as he leaned on the editor's desk.

Harris had been shuffling more papers on his desk as he was talking to Regan, but he stopped and sat down in his chair. He stared back at Regan who was for the first time showing the defiance that had made him so many enemies in the past. Harris remembered when he was like that. His strong willed actions had nearly cost him his career once, but he had learned to use them at the proper times. He hoped that Regan would also learn to use them properly.

"Sit down, Tom," said Harris.

Regan obeyed the gentle command.

"Okay, Tom," said Harris as he rested his elbows on the desk, "between you and me that attitude will not exist. You and I won't forget what's happened yesterday or the day before, but we won't let it interfere with what we have to do today. Is that clear?"

"That makes more sense to me," said Regan.

"Good," smiled Harris. "Now let's get down to business. What did you find out from Cortland?"

Regan reached into his inside coat pocket and removed the envelope that Jack Cortland had given him. He tossed it onto the desk in front of Harris.

"Inside that envelope is proof positive that Lee Harvey Oswald was in the pay of the FBI and the CIA at the time that John Kennedy was assassinated."

Harris picked up the envelope but did not open it. Instead, he fanned it a few times in front of his face.

"This thing is hotter than a pistol," said Harris.

"What else have you got?"

"Isn't that enough?"

"No, we still don't know where to find Williams, Archer, and Holman."

"Wait a minute," said Regan. "Cortland did say something about that. He said he saw a man named Phil Schramm in Ensenada, Mexico a few years ago. This Phil Schramm was the captain of a charter fishing boat, and Cortland said he did bear a resemblance to Lee Harvey Oswald."

"That's pretty good," said Harris, "but not as good as what I've got."

"Oh, yeah? What have you got?"

"Last night," said Harris as he opened the middle drawer of his desk and removed a large manila envelope, "I drove out to Youngtown to talk to Holman's mother. She told me that she hasn't seen or heard from her son in fourteen years; not since a few days after JFK was killed. She had received a letter from him the Tuesday after the assassination. She let me read it, and I'm glad I did. Do you know why?"

"Don't play games, Milt. What did it say?"

"Here," said Harris as he handed an eight-by-twelve photograph to Regan, "read it yourself."

Regan snatched the picture of a letter from the editor's hand. He read:

Dear Mom,

I hope you can use the money. It is all I have right now, but I should be coming into a lot more very soon. I am going to do this job on Friday for some very important people, and they are going to pay me a great deal of money for it. Once it is over we will both be on easy

163

street for the rest of our lives. I will tell you
more about it when I can. See you soon.

> *Love,*
> *Jimmy*

P.S. The key is to a safety deposit box of mine.
Keep it in a safe place for me. Thanx.

"This is great!" exclaimed Regan.

"There's more," said Harris as he pushed another photo toward Regan. "Here's a picture of the envelope. Note the postmark."

"Dallas, Texas, November 22, 1963," Regan read aloud. "Holy shit! This is too much to believe!"

"Still not through," grinned Harris as he held up a key. "This isn't the original, but I think it will do, don't you?"

"How'd you do it?"

"I got her to let me make a wax impression."

"No," said Regan, "I mean, how did you talk her into it?"

"I lied a lot," confessed Harris. "After she told me she hadn't seen or heard from her son since that letter, I gave her a story about how one of her neighbors had asked us to find her son for her. She fell for it."

"Hey, that wasn't very nice to mislead her like that. I mean, that seems kind of cruel to use a lonely old woman's hopes of seeing her son again."

"Hold it right there, Mister Regan," ordered Harris. "You're the one who started this whole business. You're the one who's looking for her son."

"Yeah, but . . ."

"But hell! If her son is part of the conspiracy that killed John Kennedy, then we have to prove it, no matter whose toes get stepped on."

"I suppose you're right," conceded Regan, "but I still don't like doing things that way."

"I know it isn't the best way to do things," said Harris, "but sometimes you have to be nasty in this business. I don't like stooping to such methods, but what has to be done has to be done."

"Okay, let's drop it," said Regan. "What else did you find out?"

"She has letters from her son that date back to the day he went into the Marines. I didn't read them all, but she told me that his whole career in the Marines and his career with the CIA are in them, including all of his aliases."

"That's fantastic!"

"There's more yet. She has several pictures of him, and if he isn't a dead-ringer for Oswald, I'll eat my hat."

"Praise the Lord, brother! I do believe we have a case."

"Not so fast, Tom," warned Harris. "All this still doesn't deliver Holman to us."

"Yeah, I guess you're right again. Any leads in that direction?"

"We might have one," said Harris as he removed another photograph from the manila envelope. "Remember that the only address we had for Archer was a post office box in Scottsdale? Well, Gus has had somebody watching it night and day, and only one person has been taking mail from it." He slid the photo over to Regan. "We don't know who she is yet, but the next time she comes to the box to get the mail she'll be followed."

"You won't have to go that far," said Regan. "This is Rita Bagdonovich."

"What?" exclaimed Harris. "Are you sure?"

"Positive," said Regan. "Would you forget a face and a body like that?"

"No, I guess not."

"This is Rita Bagdonovich all right," said Regan. "The same woman whose husband was killed in an automobile accident in December."

"But why would she be getting mail from Archer's box in Scottsdale?"

"Beats the hell out of me," said Regan, "but I'm sure as hell going to find out."

Regan stood up to leave.

"Hold on," said Harris. "I'm going with you."

They drove out to the house on Wagon Wheel Drive in less than thirty minutes. Regan noticed that something was different about the place as soon as they pulled up in front of it. There was a real estate sign standing in the front yard offering the house for sale. They wondered about the sign as they walked up to the front door. Harris rang the doorbell.

"Don't bother," said Regan who was peeking into a window. "The place is empty. I do believe the lady has flown the coop."

"Maybe she hasn't gone too far," said Harris as he pointed to the real estate sign. "Let's go have a chat with this real estate agent. He might know where she is."

The agency that was selling the house was on the other side of town toward Glendale. They got there just as the last salesman was locking up.

"May I help you gentlemen?" asked the pock-marked man from behind thick glasses.

"We're looking for the owner of a house on East Wagon Wheel Drive in Phoenix," said Harris as he came straight to the point. He gave the man the correct

166

address of the house.

"I'm sorry, sir," said the agent, "but we don't give out that sort of information."

Harris took two tens from his wallet.

"That's okay," said Harris. "We'll pay for it."

"It's against company policy, sir."

Harris took out a twenty.

"Now where can we find the owner?" he asked.

"I told you, sir," said the agent as he ignored the bills in Milt's hand, "we don't give out that sort of information."

"Look, friend," said Regan through clenched teeth, "if you don't tell us where we can find Rita Bagdonovich, you may find yourself on the wrong side of a court room for aiding and abetting in five murders."

"I don't know what you're talking about," protested the salesman.

"Listen, friend," said Harris, "this lady may be mixed up in several murders, and we want to find her."

"Are you the police?" he asked.

"No, we're from the newspaper," said Regan.

"If you were the police," said the salesman, "I could give you her address."

Regan grabbed him by his lapels and jerked him up and back against the door to the office.

"Listen, you stupid bastard," said Regan, "you can just pretend we're the police and give us the address."

The salesman's facial color fled from his skin causing his pockmarks to stand out even more.

"I can't do that," he pleaded.

"Yes, you can," said Regan.

"No, I can't."

"You can."

"But I'll get in trouble if I do," said the salesman.

"No, you won't," said Regan.

"Yes, I will."

"No, you won't because we won't tell if you don't."

"Let me go," said the salesman, "and I'll get her address from the files."

Regan released him, and the quivering real estate agent fumbled for his keys to unlock the door. He had it open after dropping the keys three times. He scrambled inside and went directly to the file cabinet in the rear of the office.

"How do you spell that name again?" asked the agent.

Regan spelled it for him, and the salesman found the correct folder immediately. He opened it to read the address, but Regan snatched it away from him.

"She's moved to Scottsdale," said Regan as he made a note of her address.

"Let's go," said Harris.

"Don't call the police," said Regan as he threw the file back at the salesman. "It will only get you into trouble with them as well as your boss."

"Y-y-yess-s, s-s-sir," stuttered the salesman.

It was dark when they found the apartment complex that Rita Bagdonovich had moved to in Scottsdale. The building was divided into three wings; two were perpendicular to the street and the third was in the back and parallel to the street. Rita's apartment was on the second floor of the back wing.

Harris drove his car around to the alley behind the complex. The parking stall that had Rita's apartment number over it on the facing of the carport roof was occupied by a yellow sports car. Regan made a note of the license plate number. Harris parked the car in a vacant stall, and they got out of the car. They walked around the building to the stairway at the far end. They

168

climbed to the second floor. Rita's apartment was in the center of the wing. Regan knocked on the door. It opened within seconds.

"I didn't think you would get here so soon," said Rita before she recognized Regan. "Oh, Mr. Regan. I was expecting someone else."

"Obviously not me," said Regan.

"How nice to see you again," she said.

"Yeah, I'll bet," said Regan. "You're no more glad to see me than you are the police, and that's who's going to be talking to you next if I don't get some straight answers from you."

Rita was near tears.

"Well!" snapped Regan.

"Why couldn't you leave well enough alone?" she cried. "Isn't it bad enough that Paul is dead as well as all those other people? Why don't you let it rest, Mr. Regan?"

"I can't now," said Regan. "Are you going to talk or do I call the police?"

"Come in," she said.

She held the door for them as they entered. The apartment was cluttered with packing boxes; she was either moving in or out. Regan wondered which.

"Let's start over from the beginning," said Regan. "Did your husband really get a call from a writer named Bertram?"

"Yes, that was true," she said as she sat down in an armchair. "Why don't you sit down?"

Regan and Harris sat down on the sofa, a packing box between them.

"Did he really tell you that story about Schramm and Oswald?" asked Regan.

"No, I got that information from Mr. Hewitt. He told

me about Schramm being shot by Oswald."

"Why would he tell you that?"

"He was trying to shake my memory," she said. "You know, to see if I could remember anything that Paul may have said about the incident."

"Then why did you tell me that your husband had told you that story?"

"Because I've known the truth about Paul for a long time and I didn't want it to get out. I thought if I told you he had said that then you would leave it at that, but you obviously haven't."

"No, I haven't," said Regan. "I've found out quite a few things about your husband and several other people these past few weeks. Now you tell me your version of the life and times of Paul Archer."

"Okay, I'll tell you everything," she said as she reached for her purse on the floor next to the chair.

Regan jumped up to stop her. He grabbed her arm and pulled it away from the purse.

"The last time I saw a woman reach into her purse," said Regan, "she pulled out a gun."

Regan picked up the purse.

"I was only going to get a cigarette," she said.

"Yeah, I'll bet," said Regan, "and I suppose you were going to light it with this." He held up a woman's derringer for Harris to see.

Rita hid her eyes from them.

"Nice try, lady," said Regan, "but I'm getting wise to all the tricks of the trade."

"I only carry that for self-defense."

"Sure, you do," said Regan as he pocketed her gun. He threw the purse to her. She caught it on her lap, and then she took out the cigarettes and a lighter. She flipped one cigarette from the pack and lit it.

"Paul and I met in a bar in Dallas in 1964," she said as she exhaled the blue smoke. "We had a whirlwind romance and got married a few months later. After that they started showing up."

"Who are they?" asked Regan.

"People from Paul's past," she explained. "All kinds of people; hookers, pushers, pimps, gunrunners; you name an illegal occupation and Paul knew someone in it. I never kept track of their names or their faces. Too many of them would disappear after seeing Paul."

"You mean he killed them?" asked Harris.

"No, someone else did it for him. Paul would make a long distance telephone call, and the next thing I knew I was reading how so-and-so was found dead in the desert or in a car wreck or something."

"What did these people want from Paul?" asked Regan.

"Blackmail money," said Rita as she flicked the ashes from her cigarette. "Paul used to work for Jack Ruby in Dallas. That's where he met most of those cruds."

"What did he do for Ruby?" asked Harris.

"I don't know; he would never tell me," said Rita. "I do know it had to be illegal. Why else would all those people try to blackmail him?"

"Why did he change his name to Bagdonovich?" asked Harris.

"He didn't legally. You see, when he was a boy his stepfather had it changed from Archer to Bagdonovich, which was his stepfather's last name. After he turned twenty-one, Paul had it changed back to Archer."

"So that's why his Marine Corps records say Archer instead of Bagdonovich," said Regan. "Why did he start using the name of Bagdonovich again?"

"He was trying to get away from his past. He wanted a new life with me without being reminded of his past."

"What sort of past was it?" asked Harris.

"I don't know for sure," said Rita. "I suppose he was into drugs or something. Like I said, he'd always kept that part of his life to himself."

"Did he ever tell you anything about his days in the Marines?" asked Regan.

"Not a thing."

"How about his old buddies in the Marines?" asked Harris. "Did he ever mention any of them?"

"Just your brother-in-law and some other guy he once got a letter from."

"What was the other guy's name?" asked Regan.

"I don't remember; it was so long ago. I do recall that the letter had a Mexican postmark on it. Mazsin, Mexico was the name of the place the letter came from. I've never heard of the place."

"Could you spell that?" asked Harris.

"Sure. M-A-Z-S-I-N. Mazsin.

Regan wrote the letters down in his notebook as Rita had spelled them.

"Are you sure you can't remember the guy's name who wrote the letter?" asked Regan.

"All I can remember about that letter is the postmark. Paul burned it before I could read it."

"Did Paul say anything about the guy who wrote it?" asked Regan.

"Only that they had been buddies in the Marines and that Paul owed his life to this man."

"How's that?" asked Harris.

"I don't know," said Rita. "Paul wouldn't talk about it."

"Is there anyone else you can remember?" asked

172

Regan.

"No, that's all there is."

"I guess that about does it," said Harris.

"Yeah, I suppose so," said Regan. "This is the third time someone has told us something connected with Mexico. Are you thinking what I'm thinking?"

"That maybe Holman is in Mexico?" asked Harris.

"That's right," said Regan.

"Did you say Holman?" asked Rita.

"Yes, I did," said Harris. "Does it mean anything to you?"

"That's the name that was on the letter from Mazsin," said Rita. "J. A. Holman; yes, I'm sure that was it."

"That's terrific," said Harris. "Now all we have to do is find a town called Mazsin, and we might get another lead on Holman."

"That still leaves us Williams," said Regan. "We don't know where to find him."

"He's probably right under our noses," said Harris, "and we don't know it."

"That's what scares me," said Regan as he stood up to leave.

"Well, we can worry about that later," said Harris. "Right now let's go back to my office and try to find Mazsin on a map of Mexico, and maybe Gus will have something for us, too."

"Are you going to call the police?" asked Rita.

"What for?" asked Regan. "Your husband is dead. It won't do him or the police any good now, and we've got what we want."

Regan and Harris returned to the offices of *The Morning Sun* in downtown Phoenix. Harris led Regan to a

173

room where there was a large map of Mexico hanging on a wall. They looked for a town called Mazsin, but it was not to be found on that map. They went up to the editor's office on the third floor. Harris went directly to his telephone.

"Who are you calling?" asked Regan.

"Red Starrette," said Harris as he dialed a number. "He owns a travel agency; goes to Mexico all the time. He should know where Mazsin is located."

Harris was silent as he waited for someone to answer the call on the other end.

"Hello, Ted?"

"Hi, Milt," said Starrette. "What can I do for you?"

"I'm trying to find a little town in Mexico called Mazsin. Have you ever heard of it?"

"No, I don't think so," said Starrette. "Could you spell it for me? You might be mispronouncing it."

Harris spelled it for him, and Starette let out a loud chuckle.

"What's so funny?" asked Harris.

"Where did you get that name?"

"It was postmarked on an envelope," explained Harris.

"Well, no wonder you can't find it. There's no such place."

"Then what does it mean?" asked Harris.

"That's the abbreviation from Mazatlan, Sinaloa," laughed Starrette.

"Mazatlan? Of course, why didn't I think of that? Thanks, Ted."

"Don't mention it."

The conversation came to an end.

"Mazatlan," said Harris. "Can you imagine that?"

"Okay, what about it?" asked Regan.

174

"Don't you see, Tom? Joe Paris told us that he thought he saw Holman in Acapulco."

"And Jack Cortland said he thought the Phil Schramm he met in Ensenada looked a lot like Oswald."

"Right," said Harris, "and now Rita Bagdonovich tells us about a letter from a J.A. Holman from Mazatlan. They're all towns in Mexico."

"I'll go you one better," said Regan. "Cortland said his man was a fishing boat captain, and Paris said he saw Holman on the docks."

"Right, and Mazatlan is also a fishing town. Even money says Holman is in one of those three places, and if he isn't, I'll bet he comes to one of them in the near future."

"Does this mean I get an all expense paid trip to Mexico?"

"No, it means we get an all-expense-paid-trip to Mexico. Acapulco, here we come."

Regan was not quite as excited about the trip as Harris was. He was wondering what he was going to do with Bill Davis who was waiting for him in their motel room.

"I'm going to Acapulco with Milt Harris," said Regan when he had returned to the motel. "We're leaving in the morning. We're pretty sure that Holman is there in Acapulco, or he's in Mazatlan or Ensenada. We aren't sure which one, but Milt thinks it's Acapulco. That's why we're starting there."

"What about me?" asked Davis.

"I was just coming to that," said Regan. "I think you should lay low here in Phoenix. The Vegas police aren't really looking for you anyway. At least, they aren't trying hard to find you."

"I'd rather go to Mexico with you," said Davis. "After all, I do speak the language, and you're going to need a tough hombre like me more than ever down there."

"What am I supposed to do? Tell Milt I helped a fugitive from justice with the company's money? No, you're staying here until I get back."

"Wait a minute," said Davis. "Why don't you and I go to Mazatlan while Harris goes to Acapulco? That way I could get out of here and still be your bodyguard."

"You know, you might have something there. We'd be covering two bases at the same time that way."

"Right," said Davis. "The killer has been following you, which means he's not likely to follow Harris to Acapulco unless you go with him."

"But if we went to Mazatlan," said Regan, "the killer would follow us."

"Right, and we could be waiting for him there."

"That sounds like a better idea to me," said Regan. "I'll call Milt right now and ask him what he thinks.'

Regan placed the call to the editor's residence in north Phoenix.

"Hello, Milt? This is Regan."

"I'm glad you called, Tom," said Harris. "I just had a call from Brad McCauley He said the Vegas police were able to get an old mug shot of David Williams from the Dallas police. He's going to have a copy of it made for me. It should get here in the morning."

"That's terrific," said Regan. "I'd like to get a look at the man who's been trying to kill me. Maybe I'll know who he is next time I see him."

"That isn't all," said Harris. "Brad said that he's been doing a little checking of his own, and he found out

176

that Joe Paris was importing his illegal immigrants from three different ports of call.''

"Let me guess," said Regan. "Acapulco, Mazatlan, and Ensenada.''

"How did you know?" mocked Harris. "Anyway, most of them were being paid for by some Hollywood types that are using them as servants and gardeners and such.''

"Sounds fascinating," said Regan. "Is anything being done about the illegal immigrant ring?''

"Brad said he tipped off the immigration authorities to what has been going on. It's in their hands now.''

"Good."

"I was thinking, Tom, that it might not be a good idea for you to go to Acapulco with me.''

"What? This is my show.''

"We've been through all that before," said Harris. "Let me finish, will you?''

"All right, go ahead.''

"I was thinking that we could cover two bases at one time if you were to go to Mazatlan while I went to Acapulco. We could meet up later, and then go to Ensenada together. What do you think?''

"It sounds like you're afraid the killer might kill you, too, if he saw you with me.''

"That isn't it," said Harris.

"I was only kidding," said Regan. "I think you've got a good idea there. Why not?''

"Then it's settled," said Harris.

Better than you think, thought Davis.

XII

Mazatlan

March 5, 1977

Milt Harris had had Ted Starrette make all the arrangements for his trip to Acapulco as well as Regan's trip to Mazatlan. Starrette had been very quick to complete the details. Besides making the necessary flight reservations and hotel accommodations, the travel agent had called ahead to the two Mexican cities to close friends of his. He had asked each of them to meet Harris and Regan at the airports where each one would be arriving.

Regan had called Starrette in order to have him make identical travel plans for Bill Davis. When Regan had asked the agent to keep his call a secret, Starrette had agreed, but not until Regan had told him that Davis was his bodyguard, a fact that he did not want Harris to know because he did not want Harris to worry about him.

Regan and Davis were met at the Mazatlan airport by Benito Rojas, the friendly manager of the Hotel Playa Del Rey. Rojas, who was known as Benny by all of his gringo guests and friends, was a close friend of Ted Starrette. Regan had learned from Starrette that Benny was a man who had his fingers in every tortilla in Mazatlan. More than that, Rojas was one man a stranger could trust. Regan was surprised by Benny's command of the English language; he spoke it almost without an accent.

Benny's light skin pigmentation also caught Regan off guard. Regan had almost expected a Pancho Villa to greet him at the terminal instead of a man who looked more like Clark Gable than Cesar Romero or Gilbert Roland. Only his native costume gave away Benny's nationality.

Rojas met them at the customs station inside the terminal. His presence there expedited the process of inspection. Regan was given the impression that Rojas was a man of great influence. He planned to take advantage of that asset.

"Ted Starrette said that I could safely put myself in your hands, Mr. Rojas," said Regan as soon as they were all inside the hotel's private limousine and on their way to the Playa Del Rey.

"Since you are a friend of Ted's, Mr. Regan," said Rojas, "you are also my friend. I would be pleased if you would call me Benny."

"Only if you call me Tom," said Regan.

"All right, Tom," smiled Rojas.

"Did Ted tell you why I was coming down here?" asked Regan.

"He said you would be looking for another American, a fishing boat captain," said Rojas.

"That's right," said Regan. "The man I'm looking for may be hiding from the law in the United States. I'm not sure what name he's using these days, but it might be Schramm or Holman."

"I think I know the man you are looking for," said Rojas. "There is an American named Schramm who comes to Mazatlan quite often with his boat. His home port is Acapulco."

"I was afraid of that," said Regan. "Well, Bill, it looks like Milt is going to get the brass ring."

"Maybe we ought to get back on a plane and head for Acapulco," said Davis.

"I'd better call Milt first," said Regan, "before we do. He might want me to go ahead to Ensenada. Benny, could you place a long distance call to Phoenix for me as soon as we reach the hotel?"

"With pleasure," said Benny.

"Won't he be on his way to Acapulco?" asked Davis.

"No, his plane wasn't supposed to leave till late this afternoon," said Regan. "I should be able to catch him in his office before he leaves for the airport."

It was a twenty-minute drive from the airport to the Hotel Playa Del Rey, which was situated on the bay north of the city. The building was beautifully Mexican in its architecture, but it was also quite modern. Five stories high and shaped like a square horseshoe, the Playa Del Rey was a romantic setting. It had an interior courtyard between its wings where guests could swim in a fresh water pool if they did not care to bathe in the ocean which was only a hundred yards away. The hotel offered indoor as well as outdoor dining and drinking areas, which were just off the beach.

Regan was captivated by it all with the single exception of the prices, but since he was not paying for anything with his own money, he only cared about his own comfort. Given his choice of rooms, Regan chose one of the two suites that were available that weekend. Benny took them to the one on the third floor of the north wing.

"I think you will find this suite to be very much to your liking," said Benny as he held the door for his guests. "It is not our best, of course, but it is very comfortable."

Regan and Davis walked through the three rooms of the suite inspecting it. They rejoined Rojas in the spacious drawing room.

"This is terrific," said Regan as he flopped down on the sofa.

"Did Ted advise you about our water?" asked Benny.

"If you mean Montezuma's Revenge," said Regan, "I know all about it."

"Good," said Rojas, "then I can save tourist lecture number three for some other time. Now I will make that telephone call for you."

Regan gave the number to Rojas, and in less than fifteen minutes, Milt Harris was on the line.

"Regan, what are you doing wasting my money on phone calls?" demanded Harris.

"I've got some good news for you," said Regan.

"Oh, yeah? Like what?"

"Like I . . ."

"Hold on a second, Tom," interrupted Harris. "Gus just walked in with something."

There was silence on the line.

"This is incredible!" Regan heard Harris say away from the mouthpiece of his extension. "Are you sure this is the right one?" he heard Harris ask Gus. He was unable to distinguish what Gus replied. "And you double checked this out?" heard Regan. There was a heavy sigh, probably from Harris. "This is really fantastic." Regan could imagine Harris rubbing his forehead in disbelief of whatever it was that was in front of him at the moment.

"Tom," said Harris as he returned to their conversation, "do you know who this mug shot looks like?"

"What mug shot?" asked Regan because he had forgotten that Brad McCauley was sending one of David Williams to Milt that day.

"The one McCauley sent me from Vegas," said Harris. "The one of David Williams. Can you guess who it is?"

"John Dillinger," said Regan.

"Don't be funny," snapped Harris.

"How the hell would I know who it is? You're the one who's got it."

"Hold onto your hat," warned Harris. "It's your late friend Bill Davis."

Regan choked as his mind blasted into a vacuum and his whole body went numb. The scene of the room surrounding him retreated from his view as if he was looking at it through the wrong end of a telescope. His outward aspect was almost as frightening, as all the color left his face and his eyes became glassy. It was easy to see that he had received a horrible shock, the dimensions of which even he could not judge just yet.

"Tom, are you there?" shouted Milt in his ear although to Regan it was only a distant echo.

"Uh, yeah, Milt," said Regan. "What was that you just said?"

"I said this mug shot is a picture of Bill Davis, your friend who disappeared in Vegas."

And who is now only a few feet away from me, Regan thought to himself.

"I agree," said Regan, "that is incredible."

"That isn't all," said Harris. "Gus did a little homework and found out there isn't any record of either a Paul Bagdonovich or a Paul Archer dying in an automobile accident in December or any other month for that matter."

"Are you sure?"

"As sure as I can be," said Harris. "There's one more little item you might be interested in. Rita Bag-

182

donovich disappeared from her apartment some time between last night when we were there and this afternoon when the police went over there to pick her up."

"Are they positive?" asked Regan.

"All her clothes were gone," said Harris. "I would say that the lady has skipped out with her not-so-dead husband. Since we don't know what he looks like, I was only able to give the police that picture of her to go by. There's no telling where they're at by now."

"Do you think they might come here?" asked Regan.

"That's possible," said Harris, "but the police checked the passenger list of your flight. Everyone on it checked out."

"That's good news," sighed Regan.

"They could've taken a private plane," said Milt. "The police are checking that possibility right now."

"What do you think it all means?"

"I haven't added it all up yet, but I think we'd both be wise to be on the lookout for strangers."

"I think you're right," said Regan. "Now let me tell you what I've found out so far."

"Okay, let's have it," said Harris.

"There is a fishing boat captain named Schramm who frequents this port. He's from Acapulco."

"That's great!" exclaimed Harris. "I'll be there this evening. Why don't you get a good night's sleep and meet me in Acapulco in the morning?"

"Do you mean it?" asked Regan.

"Of course, I do," said Harris. "It's your show, isn't it?"

"Well, all right, Uncle Milty!" said Regan.

"Uncle Milty? If you call me that again, you're off the payroll."

"I hear you talking," said Regan. "What a bunch of

sour grapes you can be!"

"Life is tough all over," said Harris. "Anything else you want to tell me?"

Regan's thoughts turned to the immediate problem of Bill Davis alias David Williams. Fear knifed him again.

"No, not yet," said Regan. "Call me when you get to Acapulco."

"Right," said Harris.

Regan hung up the receiver. He turned away from Davis to look out at the ocean. He was trying to keep his cool in the face of the man he was certain had tried to kill him on at least four different occasions. He began to reason it out, but Rojas interrupted his powers of deduction.

"Tom," said Benny. "I think you misunderstood me."

"Oh? How's that?"

"I said Captain Schramm's home port was Acapulco," said Rojas. "I didn't say that he was there for certain."

"That's right," said Davis. "For all we know, he might be tied up to one of the piers right here in Mazatlan."

"That is possible," said Rojas. "I can call my cousin at the Port Authority office. He will know which boats are in the harbor at this time."

Regan was silent as he was not really listening to what Rojas was saying.

"Why don't you do that?" suggested Davis.

"Yeah, go ahead," said Regan as things began to sink into his brain again.

Rojas made the call to his cousin. Their conversation was in Spanish. Regan could pick out a word here and there, but the majority of the words passed over his

184

head. Davis understood every word, and he made an effort to translate for Regan.

"His cousin is looking for a boat with a Captain Schramm on it among the boats listed as being in port this weekend."

Regan was not listening to Davis. He was still trying to sort out the information that Milt Harris had given him about the mug shot that identified Bill Davis as David Williams, the non-death of Paul Archer, and the disappearance of Rita Bagdonovich. He wondered how it all fit together.

"Benny is thanking his cousin," said Davis as he continued to interpret for Regan.

"My cousin says there is a boat named the *Agua Salada* in the harbor," said Rojas as he replaced the telephone receiver. "The captain is a man named Phil Schramm."

"That's our man," said Davis.

"How do we find this man?" asked Regan.

"I will take you down to the docks myself," said Benny. "I know exactly where his boat will be tied up."

"Terrific!" said Davis. "Let's get down there before he finds out we're here."

"Why would he be expecting us?" asked Regan.

"You can never tell about these people," said Davis as he went to his suitcase. "They have eyes and ears everywhere."

Davis opened his suitcase and removed his shaving kit. At least, Regan thought it was a shaving kit until Davis started to assemble his gun from the pieces that were concealed in the bag. Benny's eyes widened as he watched Davis at work.

"I wondered what you had done with that thing," said Regan. "That's a cute way to get it through the customs inspectors.''

"The only way," said Davis without looking up.

"What does this mean?" asked Benny.

"It's nothing to worry about, Benny," said Regan.

"Bill is my bodyguard. The man we're after may be on the dangerous side."

"That's right," said Davis, "and I don't want him to be anymore dangerous than I am."

That's for sure, thought Regan.

"I am not certain that I like this, Tom," said a nervous Benny Rojas. "This has the odor of trouble about it."

"Don't worry yourself," said Davis. "This won't involve you."

"I'd better explain a few things," said Regan as he put his arm around Benny's shoulders and guided him toward the door. "Wait here, Bill. I'll talk to Benny outside on the terrace."

The hotel manager moved cautiously with Regan out onto the balcony out of Davis's hearing range. Regan closed the door behind them before beginning any explanations. Davis continued checking out his gun to make certain that it was as ready as he was.

"Benny went down to get the car around front for us," said Regan as he stepped back inside. "Is that thing loaded?"

"She's all set and raring to go," said Davis, with a gleam in his eyes that Regan tried to avoid looking at.

"Let's hope you don't have to use that thing," said Regan as he opened the door again.

"Yeah, right," said Davis, although he was not very convincing to Regan.

They walked down the stairs instead of taking the elevator. Rojas had the limousine waiting for them when they came out of the building.

"Just a minute," said Regan before getting into the car after Davis. "I want to get some gum. It'll help calm my nerves."

"I'll show where to buy it, Tom," offered Benny as he jumped out of the driver's seat and raced around the front of the car.

They were only gone a few minutes; hardly enough time for Davis to get suspicious. Davis waited calmly in the back seat contemplating what the next few hours would bring his way.

"Sorry for taking so long," said Regan as he climbed in next to Davis.

"Hardly missed you," said Davis.

"Shall we go?" asked Rojas.

"Let's be off," said Regan feeling more confident.

The docks were only a ten-minute drive from the hotel, and Benny wasted no time getting there. He stopped the car at the end of the pier that his cousin had said the *Agua Salada* was tied up. Dozens of craft were moored to that particular dock; everything from small outboards to large commercial fishers. The pier itself was nearly deserted by people as it was still siesta time.

"The boat you are looking for is down there," said Benny as he pointed toward the end of the dock. "You can get out here and go ahead while I park the car. I will join you in a few minutes."

"Don't bother," said Davis. "We can handle this."

Benny shot a glance at Regan.

"Yeah, Benny," said Regan. "You do what you have to do, and we'll handle this."

"Whatever you say," said Rojas.

Davis was already on the dock when Regan closed the car door behind them.

"Hey, what's the hurry?" asked Regan.

"I don't want him to get away," said Davis.

"We don't even know if he's there," said Regan. "If he is, he's only two ways to go. If he comes this way we'll get him. If he heads out to sea, we'll grab another boat and go after him."

Davis slackened his pace. The wooden pier clunked beneath their feet as they approached the *Agua Salada*. The forty-foot cabin cruiser was far from being on its last legs. Its white finish and deep blue trim needed to be touched up with a fresh coat of paint, but the hull itself appeared to be in decent shape. The size of the boat told Regan that its owner had used a fair piece of change to purchase it new or used.

"Anyone here?" called out Regan as they stopped on the pier alongside the craft.

"Don't bother with that," said Davis as he boarded the boat. "Let's have a look around."

The after deck was free of equipment and chairs for fishermen. Everything was neatly stowed in its proper place. The bridge was above the cabin. In front of the wheel, Regan saw a director's chair with the name "Capt. Schramm" on the back of the cloth crosspiece. The door to the cabin was closed. It opened, and a sandy-haired man with a darker shade of brown beard stepped out on the deck.

"Can I help you?" he asked as he shaded his eyes from the glaring sunlight.

"Yes, I hope so," said Regan as he was still sizing up this skinny man in faded dungarees, red and white striped tee-shirt, and white deck shoes. "We're looking for Captain Schramm."

"I'm Captain Schramm," he said.

"And I'm the Lone Ranger," said Davis.

"Williams!" gasped the captain as he backed away from Davis toward the cabin.

"Hold it right there, Jimmy," warned Davis as he pulled his gun from his waistband. "Get out here in the middle of the deck where I can keep a close eye on you."

"What're you doing, Bill?" asked Regan as if he was unaware of what was transpiring.

"Don't be stupid, Tom," said Davis. "This bird is Jimmy Holman."

"Yes, I guessed that," said Regan, "but why the gun?"

"Jimmy Holman is a thoroughly dangerous man," said Davis. "Treacherous, too."

"Why did he call you Williams?" asked Regan.

"Because that's who he is," said the captain.

"That's right, Tom. I'm David Williams, one of the three men you've been looking for. This bastard is number two, and number three is dead."

"Hold it," said Regan as he sat down on the starboard siding. "I don't understand all of this. Would you mind filling in a few of the gaps?"

"I suppose it won't make any difference now," said Davis, alias Williams, as he turned his back to the cabin door, "but first I think we'd better get started for the open sea. Get up there, Holman."

He waved his gun at Holman motioning him to climb up to the bridge. The captain stepped past Regan toward the ladder. Regan watched him grab the top two rungs, then he saw the barrel of a shotgun protrude from the cabin doorway.

"Not so fast, Williams," said a voice from inside the compartment.

"Archer!" said the startled Williams, alias Davis, as

189

he turned to face his enemy.

"Stop right there!" warned the man in the cabin. "Toss that gun over the side."

Williams hesitated, but the proximity of the business end of the shotgun to his ribs convinced him to obey.

"That's a good boy," said Archer. "Now you and Mr. Regan march yourselves down here while the captain gets us underway."

The shotgun retreated inside the door, and Williams and Regan followed it single file. The captain went forward then aft to cast off the lines that secured the *Agua Salada* to the pier. Just as quickly, he was topside again starting the engine.

The light in the compartment was not conducive to recognizing everything immediately. As Regan's eyes adjusted, he saw that the cabin was very spacious. A table dominated the left side of the room, and a bench seat ran along the bulkhead on the right. Another door in the forward wall was flanked by bookshelves. The books were held in place by restraining bars, and Regan thought it was odd that nearly all the books had something to do with John Kennedy, Lee Harvey Oswald, and Jack Ruby.

"Sit down over there," said Archer.

Regan looked back over his shoulder to see the tall dark man pointing the shotgun toward the bench. Without hesitation, Regan flopped down on the seat remaining as casual as possible. Williams sat down beside him. Archer rested his buttocks on the edge of the table as he stood facing his prisoners.

"Well, Mr. Regan," said Archer, "You've led me on a merry chase."

"Do you mean you've been following me?" asked Regan trying to act as surprised as he could.

"You know," said Archer, "for a reporter, you sure are stupid."

"I am a newspaper writer," corrected Regan.

"Same difference," shrugged Archer. "You're still a dummy. If you'd had any brains at all, you would've checked out Rita's story about me being killed in an automobile accident. When you didn't, I figured you for a sucker until you went to Salt Lake and found Hewitt. That's when I figured you had to die."

"Then you're the one who killed the kid in Oregon," said Regan.

"That's right," confirmed Archer. "I thought he was you. It was too dark to see that he was just a kid. At least he died quick and clean."

"You were the one outside Hewitt's that night," said Regan, "weren't you?"

"Right again," smiled Archer, his lips twisted. "When I found out you were still alive, I couldn't believe it. You must have nine lives."

"I do get lucky now and then," said Regan.

"I still haven't figured out how you got away from that whore in Vegas," said Archer. "She was sure damned surprised to see me standing there at the elevator."

"Were you the man with the camera in Disneyland?" asked Regan.

"How in the hell did you pick me out of that crowd? I was sure you wouldn't see me."

"If you hadn't run," said Regan, "I would've told Cortland to forget about you."

"I'll be damned," laughed Archer.

"I would've caught you in the parking lot if that station wagon hadn't gotten in the way."

"It's lucky for you again, Mr. Regan," said Archer.

191

"If you had caught me, I would've killed you then."

"You must've had lots of chances to kill me along the way," said Regan. "Why didn't you try in Phoenix?"

"Two reasons. You always had that editor of yours with you or you were with Williams here. The other is I figured you'd follow up on that tip Rita gave you, which would make it easier for me to get rid of you two down here. The Mexican police don't ask too many questions when a couple of gringos are found dead."

The boat began rolling as it reached the open sea. Regan was beginning to feel giddy, which meant he would soon be sick to his stomach from the motion of the boat being tossed by the waves.

"I still don't understand all this," said Regan. "Now let me get this straight. You're Paul Archer alias Paul Bagdonovich, the guy who was supposed to have been killed in an automobile wreck in December. Am I right?"

"You're batting a thousand so far," said Archer.

"And this guy next to me is David Williams alias Bill Davis."

"You're still perfect," said Archer.

"And the guy at the helm is Jimmy Holman alias Phil Schramm, right?"

Archer's lips twisted into that maniacal smile of his as he shook his head from side to side.

"Two out of three aint bad, Mr. Regan," said Archer.

"Two out of three?"

"That's right, Mr. Regan. Two out of three."

Archer backed over to the door, the shotgun still pointing at Williams.

"I don't get it," said Regan.

"Tell Mr. Regan down here who you are," shouted Archer to the man topside.

"I'm a dead man," the captain shouted back.

Archer guffawed at the irony of the captain's words.

"What's so funny?" demanded Williams.

"Williams, you always were a little slower than most," said Archer. "Don't you know who that is up there?"

"Of course, I do," said Williams. "He's Jimmy Holman, the same sonofabitch that helped you steal my dough."

"You're right about one thing," said Archer. "He did steal your cut, but he aint Jimmy Holman."

"Then who the hell is he?" asked Regan.

"Mr. Regan, that man up there is none other than Lee Harvey Oswald," said Archer, before he let loose with another loud roar of laughter.

Regan was incredulous; he could not believe his ears. Archer was crazy, or so Regan thought.

"You're out of your mind, Archer," said Williams. "Jack Ruby killed Oswald in Dallas fourteen years ago."

"Did he, Williams? Think back to that day in Dallas; not the day Ruby shot a man, but the day we killed Kennedy."

"You killed President Kennedy?" said Regan.

"You are a jerk, Mr. Regan," said Archer. "Of course, we killed Kennedy; the three of us: Williams, Holman, and me. We shot him, didn't we, Williams?"

"That's right, we did," said Williams, "only I didn't get paid for it. You and Holman stole my dough."

"I told you already, Williams, that is not Holman up there. He's Lee Harvey Oswald. Holman's dead; Ruby killed him, not Oswald."

"That's impossible," said Regan. "Thirty-five million people saw Jack Ruby shoot Lee Harvey Oswald."

"Wrong, Mr. Regan. They saw a man who looked just like Oswald being murdered by Ruby. That man was Jimmy Holman."

"You're crazy, Archer," said Williams.

"I don't want to hear you say that again!" growled Archer. "You weren't there, so shut up and listen."

"Go ahead with your story," interjected Regan.

"Like I was saying," said Archer in a calmer tone, "that day in Dallas when we killed Kennedy, Williams was on the knoll behind the fence. I was on top of the Criminal Courts Building, and Holman was in the Book Depository. Remember that, Williams? Sure you do. We would've had a perfect crime if you hadn't fired first. No one would have every suspected a thing if you had only waited another five seconds. You dumb-ass! Because of you . . ."

"Don't point the finger at me," said Williams. "You were the one who killed that cop and then let everyone in the whole world see you."

"The stupid bastard had it coming," said Archer. "If he'd gone to the theater like he was supposed to, he'd be a hero today instead of in a grave. I had to kill him, or he would've sold us out."

"Then what happened?" interjected Regan.

"What do you want to know for?" snarled Archer. "You aint going to get to write about it."

"Let's just call it curiosity," said Regan.

"Curiosity killed the cat," said Archer, and then he started laughing at his own morbid joke. Regan and Williams were not laughing with him.

"Very funny," said Regan.

"Don't get smart with me, Mr. Regan," snapped Archer. "I can kill you now as well as later."

"Good point," said Regan, "but I think you want to

194

satisfy my curiosity before you do. Am I right?''

"Clever sonafabitch, aren't you?'' said Archer.

"I try,'' replied Regan.

"Okay, I'll tell you what happened. After the shooting, we all went to our respective points of rendezvous. From there, I went to meet the cop to tell him where he could find Oswald; only the cop had different ideas. He was going to arrest me. He left me no choice; I had to shoot him. I took off because there were people all over the place. I ran until Holman spotted me. He picked me up, and we drove around for a few minutes before deciding that we had to kill Oswald ourselves. We went to the theater. Since I had already been seen by too many people, we decided that he should go in after Oswald. I drove around back and waited for him; only he didn't come out. Holman was still inside looking for Oswald when the cops showed up. I hightailed it out of there and came back ten minutes later. I was driving around the block when I saw Oswald walking toward the theater. It was then that I knew that the cops had caught Holman. I picked up Oswald, telling him that there had been a change in plans. We were heading over to meet Ruby when it dawned on me that I was the only one who knew that the cops had grabbed the wrong guy. I decided not to tell anyone. I just headed the car for the airport like we were supposed to do. Williams hadn't gotten there yet, so I told the pilot and the payoff man that the cops had grabbed him. We were in the air a few minutes later.

"We had to turn around and fly back over the airport once we were up. That's when the payoff man saw Williams drive up. He pulled a gun on me as he realized that I was trying to pull a fast one. Oswald jumped him before he could do anything. He saved my life; that's why I've kept his secret all these years. He kept denying he was Oswald all the way to Phoenix. I still laugh when I think about it. Imagine him trying to tell me he wasn't Oswald.''

"What happened when you got to Phoenix?" asked Regan.

"We split the dough, and then we caught a flight to Acapulco. After being there a week, I decided it was time we went back to the States, but Oswald wanted to stay there. I didn't care, so I came back on my own."

"And I've been looking for you ever since," said Williams.

"Now that you've found me," said Archer, "what're you going to do about it?"

"Given an even chance," said Williams, "I'd tear you apart."

"So you would, David," said Archer, "but you aren't going to get an even chance."

"You haven't changed, Paul," said Williams. "You're still the same cold-blooded bastard you always were."

"I've had about enough out of you," snapped Archer. "It's time we were ending this little party. Get your ass out on deck."

Archer waved the shotgun toward the hatch, and Williams got up to go outside. The boat had been rolling considerably since it had been on the open sea. Regan had been feeling every pitch of the bow as the boat cut through the swells.

"You, too, Mr. Regan," said Archer.

"I don't think so," said Regan. "I'll puke if I have to get up."

"That's tough shit, Mr. Regan," grinned Archer as he relished the torment Regan was going through. He swung the end of the shotgun into his face. "Move it, Mr. Regan."

Williams looked back over his shoulder from the doorway to see that Archer was not paying attention to him. He turned and attacked Archer who turned just as quickly to meet the challenge. Williams grabbed the shotgun and pushed Archer backwards against the door to the sleeping compartment. The barrel lurched upward discharging a slug into the overhead. The blast went through the wood as if it was paper. They continued to struggle, and the barrel was swung down to the deck where it fired again ripping a hole through the planks. A third shot rang out splintering the bulkhead next to Regan's feet.

Regan decided it was time he did something to save his own neck, even if it was wrong. He pulled the gun that Benny Rojas had given him at the hotel from his waistband. He aimed it at the two men who were still fighting for the shotgun. With both hands clutching the grip of the .38, he followed them around the cabin with one man, then the other coming into his sights.

"All right!" shouted Regan. "I've got a gun, so drop the rifle."

They ignored him.

"I've got a gun!" he shouted again.

They still ignored him.

"Oh, shit!" said Regan aloud. "Now what, Tommy?"

Williams appeared to be winning the struggle as he was the stronger of the two men, but Archer's maniacal strength was equal to his. They strained every muscle in their life or death battle. The gun fired through the deck beneath their feet again. The explosion seemed to give Williams the edge as he gave a final heave at the gun and wrenched it away from Archer, but he also managed to jerk the shotgun over his head and out onto the after deck. Both men scrambled for it. As they collided at the door, Williams threw an elbow into Archer's jaw knocking him back inside the compartment. Williams crawled out on deck and seized the shotgun. Archer went for the gun he had in his waistband. Williams wheeled to face Archer in time to catch the first of three bullets in his chest. The shots knocked him backwards as he fired the shotgun into the air. The second bullet pushed him back against the stern, and the shotgun discharged again. A third shot was carefully placed in his chest by Archer as Williams slumped to the deck, his life over. His killer continued pointing his revolver at him until he was certain that Williams was dead.

Regan was unsure of where he was as the gunsmoke increased his nausea. Everything was happening too fast for him to follow. He felt he was retreating into a dark movie house where he was seeing a gangster film in deadly color. He was not even aware of the gun that he still held in his hands. It was directed at the back of Archer's head, which was beginning to turn slowly to face Regan.

"And now it's your turn, Mr. Regan," said Archer before he saw the gun stuck in his nose.

The crazed glint in Archer's eyes terrified Regan, who was unaware that he had the drop on Archer. His hands shook visibly, and beads of perspiration boiled up on his forehead and cheeks.

Archer saw the gun that was only inches from his face. He could see that Regan was near panic. He decided it would be best if he let Regan have the upper hand for the moment. He dropped his gun and backed away, blocking the door. Regan got to his feet, instinctively following him toward the after deck.

"I guess you win, Mr. Regan," said Archer, with that twisted grin Regan had seen so many times before.

The sound of someone speaking aroused his senses, but the explosion of the shotgun once more sent his mind reeling. Archer flew toward him as if he had been shot out of a cannon. The collision knocked Regan to the deck with Archer sprawled on top of him. Regan screamed as he threw his attacker off of him. He scrambled to one corner with the .38 still held in his right hand. He pointed it at Archer who lay motionless in the middle of the deck, a pool of blood beginning to form around his head.

Regan continued sitting there as the horror of what he was witnessing wreaked havoc with his senses. Then the sound of something thudding on the after deck saved him from total terror. His head convulsed toward the noise, and then he remembered the third man who had been at the wheel all this time. He pushed himself up using the wall as a support for his back. The deck beneath his feet rolled, and Regan slid to his right giving him a full view through the doorway at the after deck. Sweat fell in his eyes blurring his vision; he wiped it away.

The third man was lying face down just outside the door; the shotgun still smoking between him and the deck. Williams was propped up against the stern, the sun and wind drying his blood. Regan stumbled toward the door. He continued to aim the gun in his hand at the third man. He bounced off the bulkhead as he passed through the hatch. He knelt down beside the third man. He rolled him over to get a good look at his face.

"We're all dead," gasped the dying man. He laughed, then choked as blood spilled from the corners of his mouth, a gaping hole in his stomach, apparently from one of the shots Williams got off, pouring his blood on the deck. "It's too funny for words," he gurgled. "We're all dead."

A death sigh bubbled on his lips.

Regan stood up, then lunged toward the side as his seasickness and the gore of the scene finally made him wretch his guts out. He heaved until there was nothing left inside him but cramps, and then he heaved again. It cleared his head long enough for him to regain control of his senses. He turned to survey his situation.

The engine was not running. One of the shotgun blasts had gone through it shattering the distributor. Water was leaking into the cabin. It was a slow leak; there was no need to panic yet. Three dead men, one of which knew how to pilot the craft, were strewn about. He was alive; at least, Regan hoped he was.

The radio, thought Regan. Where's the radio?

He went below to look for it. It was not there.

It must be on the bridge, he thought.

He climbed topside. The radio was there. He grabbed the microphone and pushed the button to talk.

"May-day, may-day," he said calmly. "May-day, may-day."

There was no response, not even static. He checked to make sure the radio was on. It was.

"Oh, shit!" he swore as he saw the holes in the deck. "You sonofabitch! You killed the radio, too."

He pounded it with his fist as if he could make the apparatus work that way. It only made his knuckles bleed.

"Now what the hell do you do, Regan?" he asked.

He leaned over the wheel and banged his head on his clenched fists in an effort to stimulate his mind into finding a way out of this predicament. He opened his eyes and scanned the horizon.

"You wait, you lucky bastard," he said aloud, a smile parting the whiskers on his lips.

Closing in on the *Agua Salada*, Regan could see another boat with a little Mexican named Benny Rojas waving at him from the bow.

XIII

Tulsa

April 2, 1977

"Good Lord, Tommy," said Colleen, "you're lucky to be alive."

Regan was sitting across the table from his sister and brother-in-law, Dave O'Toole, in their kitchen. They were just finishing the last of the series of articles Regan had written for *The Morning Sun* about his recent investigation.

"You can say that again," said Regan as he stirred his coffee.

"I can't believe Paul Bagdonovich was really involved in all this," said Dave. "I remember him bein' a little wild when we were in the Marines, but I'd never figure him for a cold-blooded killer."

"That shows you how wrong you can be about people," said Regan. "I didn't think Bill Davis was a killer, but he was. How can you tell when you're dealing with people like that?"

"I see what you mean," said Dave.

"Has Mom seen these yet, Tommy?" asked Colleen.

"Yeah, she yelled at me already," said Regan. "All that bull about living dangerously. It was all I could do to calm her down."

"Just imagine," said Dave, "Lee Harvey Oswald alive after all these years."

"And to think it was a picture that you'd taken years

202

ago that started it all," said Colleen as she put her hand over her husband's. "And to think that my own brother found him."

"Hold it," said Regan. "The article says that Archer claimed the captain of the boat was Oswald. It doesn't say that he was. Remember, Williams said he was Jimmy Holman."

"Well, was he Lee Harvey Oswald?" asked Colleen.

Regan leaned back in his chair, a grin spread wide across his face. He coupled his hands behind his head.

"Which one was he?" asked Colleen again.

Regan's smile broadened, if that was possible.

"When you figure it out," said Regan, "you tell me."

PRIME TIME　　　　　　　　**LB499-2 $1.95**
James Kearney　　　　　　　　　　　　Novel

The book that picks up where *Network* left off . . . The
explosive novel of violent power struggles inside a
giant television network. The United Television
Network. Outside an austere glass facade . . . inside a
seething hot bed of ambitious men and women whose
motto was "show your rivals no mercy" . . . men and
women who would get what they wanted at any cost.
(Foil cover)

FLAME IN A HIGH WIND　　　**LB500-X $1.50**
Jacqueline Kidd　　　　　　　　　Adventure

A Powerful novel of romance and adventure on the
high seas. The War of 1812 ended for all but Capt.
Denny Poynter. Branded pirate, pursued by British
and Americans alike, he fought and plundered his
way around the world. But his reckless freedom
would be soon jeopardized as his first lady, the sea,
gave way to the fiery Renee.

THAT COLLISION WOMAN　　**LB501-8 $1.95**
Deidre Stiles　　　　　　　　　　　　Novel

Fleur Collison was known as the most beautiful and
wilful woman in all England. The young English-
woman would return to her ancestral home of
Ravensweir despite the fact that it was inhabited by
her former lover, now brother-in-law. She was determined to take what she wanted from the world . . .
and her sister.

ELENA　　　　　　　　　　　　**LB502-6 $1.50**
Emily Francis　　　　　　　　　　　Mystery

The commune on this small Greek island lived a
placid life among ancient monuments and clear blue
sea until Elena came. They gave her friendship and
love. She brought them death.

HOW TO DIVORCE YOUR WIFE
Forden Athearn

LB503-4 $1.95

Nonfiction

Practical advice for men from an experienced divorce lawyer, Forden Athearn on what to do before you tell your wife, how to tell your wife, family, boss, how to select a lawyer, and more!

DAY OF THE COMANCHEROS
Steven C. Lawrence

LB504-2 $1.50

Western

Slattery had witnessed the rape, murder, and pillage by the savage Comancheros but it wasn't personal until they put him on the end of a rope. No one dared stop them. Someone had to.

KILLER SEE, KILLER DO
Jonathan Wolfe

LB505-0 $1.50

Mystery

It started out as an innocent Halloween party. But innocent soon turned to bizarre when the treats stopped and a trick involving voodoo brought death to the scene. Someone was jailed and Indian detective Ben Club meant to set him free.

GUNSMOKE
Wade Hamilton

LB506-9 $1.50

Western

Ben Corcoran had become boss of Sageville range by killing anyone who tried to settle. When the quiet gambler came to town no one took notice . . . until he led the farmers in bloody revolt. First Time in Paperback.

THE LIFE OF KIT CARSON LB474ZK $1.25
John S.C. Abbott Golden West Series

Christopher "Kit" Carson was a legend to his coun-
trymen. Trapper, trailblazer, scout, and Indian
fighter, Kit Carson would become part of American
history at its most exciting time—the pioneering of
the wild west.

**THE YOKE AND
THE STAR** LB475TK $1.95
Tana de Gamez Novel

"This tense, compassionate novel has an animal
warmth and female ferocity that is very moving
indeed."

—Kirkus Review

"Expert story-telling, excitement and suspense."
—Publishers Weekly

Cuba was ready to explode into bloody revolution.
Hannan, the American newsman, could feel the
tension in the air, in the eyes of the people in the
streets and cafes. Everybody was taking sides; there
could be no neutrals in the coming conflict. Hannan
thought he could stay out of it. He was wrong. Love
for a beautiful revolutionary pushed him past the
point of no return.

**THE RETURN OF
JACK THE RIPPER** LB476KK $1.75
Mark Andrews Novel

An English acting company opened a Broadway play
based on the bloody Ripper murders of 1888. Just
as the previews began, a prostitute was found dead
in a theatre alley—disembowelled, her throat
slashed. Other murders followed, and soon the city
was gripped in terror. Had the most monstrous figure
in the annals of crime returned to kill again?

THE RED DANIEL
Duncan MacNeil

LB477DK $1.50
Adventure

The Royal Strathspey's, Britain's finest regiment, are dispatched to South Africa to take command in the bloody Boer War and find the most fabulous diamond in all of South Africa—The Red Daniel.

SLAVE SHIP
Harold Calin

LB478KK $1.75
Adventure

This is the story of Gideon Flood, a young romantic who sets sails on a slave ship for a trip that would change his life. He witnesses the cruelty of African chieftains who sell their own for profit, the callousness of the captains who throw the weak overboard, and his own demise as he uses an African slave and then sells her.

A SPRING OF LOVE
Celia Dale

LB479KK $1.50
Novel

"A fascinating story." --

—*The Washington Star*

"An immaculate performance . . . unsettling, and quite touching."

—*Kirkus Review*

This sweeping novel chronicles a determined young woman's search for enduring love. No matter where it took her, she followed her heart. The man with whom she linked her fortunes was said to be dangerous, but she knew there could be no one else.

TIME IS THE SIMPLEST THING
Clifford D. Simak

LB480DK $1.50
Science Fiction

Millions of light years from Earth, the Telepathic Explorer found his mind possessed by an alien creature. Blaine was a man capable of projecting his mind millions of years into time and space. But that awesome alien penetrated his brain, and Blaine turned against the world . . . and himself.

SEND TO: LEISURE BOOK
P.O. Box 270
Norwalk, Connecticut 06852

Please send me the following titles:

Quantity	Book Number	Price
_____	_____	_____
_____	_____	_____
_____	_____	_____
_____	_____	_____
_____	_____	_____

In the event we are out of stock on any of your selections, please list alternate titles below.

_____	_____	_____
_____	_____	_____
_____	_____	_____
_____	_____	_____

Postage/Handling _____

I enclose . . . . . . _____

FOR U.S. ORDERS, add 35¢ per book to cover cost of postage and handling. Buy five or more copies and we will pay for shipping. Sorry no C.O.D.'s.

FOR ORDERS SENT OUTSIDE THE U.S.A.
Add $1.00 for the first book and 25¢ for each additional book. PAY BY foreign draft or money order drawn on a U.S. bank, payable in U.S. ($) dollars.
☐ Please send me a free catalog.

NAME_____
(Please print)

ADDRESS_____

CITY _____ STATE _____ ZIP _____
Allow Four Weeks for Delivery